"Maybe your opinion of me matters."

His hand still on her wrist, he tugged her closer and rose from his seat. Their legs brushed and she lifted her gaze to his. Crickets chirped and tree branches rustled in the breeze, caressing the quiet night. "Casey?"

A wayward strand of hair fell into her eyes. It was always doing that—giving the wholesome, sweet girl a sexy edge—another reminder that she was all woman now. Lifting his hand, he brushed the hair onto her cheek. His fingers lingered on the softest skin he'd ever felt. It would be so easy to kiss her again. "Maybe I want you to like me for purely selfish reasons."

Her head tilted to the side and her lids lowered as she eyed his mouth. The hungry look on her face nearly blinded him. "But that means... Are you going to kiss me again, Casey?"

* * *

Redeeming the CEO Cowboy is part of The Slades of Sunset Ranch. The sun never sets on love and redemption for these rich Nevada ranchers!

* * *

If you're on Twitter
tell us what you think of Harlequin Desire!
#harlequindesire

Dear Reader,

Thanks to your loyalty, The Slades of Sunset Ranch series was extremely well received and has been a fan favorite. Since Casey Thomas was introduced in *Sunset Seduction* (Luke and Audrey's story), I've been getting requests and questions from readers asking if Casey would have a story of his own.

The answer is *yes!*

As I was writing Casey, I realized this hunky heartthrob secondary character needed a story of his own. He was just too delicious a hero not to find his own great love. He had a lot of good things going for him, and though he came on super strong protecting his sister in *Sunset Seduction,* the tables are now turned on Casey. In *Redeeming the CEO Cowboy,* his sister asks him to do her this one giant favor that involves Susanna Hart, her good friend and hometown neighbor, owner of Sweet Susie's Pastries and More. It's something Casey feels honor bound to do.

But Audrey doesn't know what she's really asking of her big brother.... Casey and Susanna share a secret that neither of them want revealed. It's difficult for Casey to help Susanna when she's barely talking to him. But Casey is a good guy at heart, and Susie and her three-year-old charge, Ally, are a hard combination for this CEO Cowboy to dismiss. They say redemption is good for the soul, right? Casey Thomas gets a dose and then some.

Warning: *This story might make you crave cupcakes!*

That's all I'm saying....

Happy reading!

Charlene

REDEEMING THE CEO COWBOY

CHARLENE SANDS

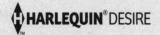
HARLEQUIN® DESIRE

Recycling programs
for this product may
not exist in your area.

ISBN-13: 978-0-373-73333-0

REDEEMING THE CEO COWBOY

Copyright © 2014 by Charlene Swink

This edition published by arrangement with Harlequin Books S.A.

For questions and comments about the quality of this book, please contact us at CustomerService@Harlequin.com.

Printed in U.S.A.

Books by Charlene Sands

Harlequin Desire

Silhouette Desire

Harlequin Historical

Other titles by this author available in ebook format.

CHARLENE SANDS

is a *USA TODAY* bestselling author of thirty-five romance novels, writing sensual contemporary romances ~~and stories~~ of the Old West. Her books have been honored with a Nat~~ional~~ Readers' Choice Award, a CataRomance Reviewers' Choice Award, and she's a double recipient of the Booksellers' Best Award. She belongs to the Orange County chapter and the Los Angeles chapter of RWA.

Charlene writes "hunky heroes with heart." She knows a little something about true romance—she married her high school sweetheart! When not writing, Charlene enjoys sunny Pacific beaches, great coffee, reading books from her favorite authors and spending time with her family. You can find her on Facebook and Twitter. Charlene loves to hear from her readers! You can write her at P.O. Box 4883, West Hills, CA 91308, or sign up for her newsletter for fun blogs and ongoing contests at www.charlenesands.com.

To Don, the sweet, wonderful man I married many, many moons ago.

Happy Special Anniversary, Sweetheart!

One

As soon as Susanna Hart spotted the chrome-rimmed Cadillac SUV turning the corner and barreling down the street, her heart fisted deep in her chest. She had known this day would come. Casey Thomas was back in town.

She held her cousin Ally's small hand and watched as the fairy-tale princess ball rolled to a stop at the front lawn of Casey's childhood home. Why wasn't she graced with good luck and timing the way some women were? She darted a glance at her front door thirty feet away. It was too late to make a mad dash. The roar of the engine mellowed. He wasn't far now. Thorny blades of grass pinched her bare toes where she stood like an immovable statue under the afternoon sun. Her palms began to sweat. She wiped her free hand on her denim jeans. "Oh, no," she muttered.

Ally's gaze immediately lifted to hers. Susanna fixed her lips into a pretend smile, scooped up the ball and handed it to the two-year-old. "Here you go, Muffin."

The worry on Ally's face crumbled and she giggled. "I'm not a muffin." She hugged the ball to her chest and announced, "I *bakeded* muffins, Auntie."

Susanna tapped a finger to the side of her mouth. "Oh, yeah, that's right. I forgot. You're my best helper."

Ally's smile widened. Poor kid. Ever since Ally had

come to live with her one month ago, she'd tried to find ways to put the child at ease and let her know she was wanted and loved. Little Ally had enough on her plate without worrying about her Aunt Susie's sudden panic right now.

Even if Susanna hadn't recognized the blond-haired breaker of her heart, Casey Thomas, commandeering the wheel of the custom-painted glossy black SUV, she would've guessed it was him. Flashy cars such as his didn't belong on Meadow Drive in the Reno suburbs. Neither did *he,* anymore.

But as he drove his SUV into the driveway of his childhood home and cut the engine, there was no mistaking the man who'd taken her virginity nearly ten years ago.

Susanna stood rooted to the spot spinning thoughts of nonchalance in her head. She'd seen Casey a few times in the last ten years. This shouldn't be so darned hard. They could simply pretend the whole taking-her-virginity incident never happened, like they did when he'd come to pay his respects at her father's funeral. Like they did when Casey broke his back riding rodeo and Susanna, being Audrey's best friend, went with his sister to pay him a visit in the hospital. Like they did when they'd bumped into each other at Sunset Ranch after Audrey had her beautiful baby girl, Ava Kasey Slade.

The driver's door opened and a beagle-size mutt scurried over Casey's lap and leapt onto the driveway. Ally's arms fluttered excitedly. "Doggy!"

The pup raced over to her, his peachy-blond tail wagging like crazy.

"Charger!" Casey's voice boomed.

Susanna swept Ally off the ground and into her arms. It wasn't the puppy's enthusiasm so much as Casey's tone that lodged a threat in her mind.

"Sorry," Casey said, lowering his voice. "He's actually

pretty harmless. Just too darn rambunctious." He hinged his body out of the SUV, his movements fractionally slower than when he was younger, before he'd broken his back in the rodeo ring. As he straightened to his full six-foot-two height, his jaw tightened. Back in the day, he saved that look for his sister Audrey when she'd done something wrong. Susanna wondered what put that look on his face today. Was he annoyed at the dog? Or was it residual pain from his injury causing him to frown? "I didn't want him to frighten the child. Come here, dog."

The puppy's tail nosedived between his legs and he trotted toward Casey.

The pup and Casey had two things in common: lush shaggy blond hair and mischievous eyes. Casey strode to where the grass met the driveway, treating it like a barrier between them. "Hello, Susanna."

Her toes curled deeper into the prickly grass. From what she could tell, Casey's former life as a rodeo champion was gone now. Dressed in a russet brown shirt tucked into beige trousers, he was still ruggedly handsome if not a little more refined. Sunlight poured over his tanned face and charming white smile. "Hello."

He cocked his head to one side. "Guess we're going to be neighbors again."

Temporarily. When she'd spoken to Audrey, she hadn't been sure when Casey would arrive, but that he'd be staying a month, maybe two. On business. Secretly, Susanna had died inside hearing the news, but couldn't let on to her best friend how much being neighbors again with her super successful, gorgeous brother distressed her.

"I guess so."

He nodded, his stark gaze piercing through barriers with unspoken words. Words she didn't want to hear. Words that were better off unsaid. "Uh, this is Ally. She lives with me now." She hugged Ally close and brushed her lips to the top of her head. Soft blond wisps tickled her mouth. "Say hello to Casey, Ally."

Ally's eyes shifted from the pup to the pup's owner. "Hello."

Casey came closer, stepping over the grass barrier, and smiled wide. "Hi, Ally." He took her hand and gave it a gentle shake. "Nice to meet you."

Ally turned back to Charger. "I like your doggy."

Charger rose up on his hind legs and pawed at Casey's expensive dress pants, a mewling sound grounding from his little throat. "I think he likes you too."

"Can I petted him?"

"That's up to…" Casey turned to Susanna with a question on his lips.

"*Aunt* Susie," she confirmed with a nod. She wasn't really Ally's aunt, but now wasn't the time for explanations. "I think it'd be all right."

Casey bent to pick up the puppy and Ally put her hand out ever so gently to stroke the puppy's head. "He's soft."

"He is," Casey said.

Lime and musk filled her nostrils. His scent reminded her of the last time they'd been this close. In the Thomas's house, on the sofa, his arms strong and sure around her as she'd cried her eyes out. The images came through clearly as if they'd happened yesterday. Ten years later, and Casey still made her heart race.

If only he wasn't going to live directly next door to her. If only he wasn't Audrey's brother. If only pressing business didn't bring him back to Reno. Susanna gave herself a mental slap. The *if onlys* had to go. Casey Thomas was here for a short time and she'd have to deal with it, just like she'd dealt with everything else in her life. On her own terms.

"The street looks the same," he said, glancing around.

"It is, for the most part." She lived in a *middle,* middle class neighborhood, the homes groomed and tidy, but missing the fancy renovations upper middle income could provide. "Mrs. Martinez moved out. She's living in a retirement home now. Peter Albertson got married right out of high school, but his mom and dad are still living here."

"That so? I'll have to stop over and say hello to Randy and Linda."

Susanna smiled. "They'd like that. I think they miss Peter a lot."

Casey glanced at his own house. No one had lived in it since Audrey moved out a year ago. Susanna watched over the property and made sure the gardener came twice a month to keep the lawn groomed.

"You still have a spare key?" Casey asked.

Susanna blinked. The question came out of left field. "Yes, do you want it back?"

Casey took in her sharp reaction and smiled slightly. "No, ma'am. I need to borrow it." He set the pup down on the grass. "I left my place in Tahoe this morning without my key. Didn't realize it until about twenty minutes ago."

Whoops. Her shrewish answer had come out of left field. She'd barked at him as if she was the canine on the property. "Oh, of course. I'll go get it for you. Come on, Ally."

Ally pushed against Susanna's chest and threw her body weight toward the dog, pointing her index finger. "Charger. Charger."

"We'll come right back, sweetie."

"I'll watch her," Casey said. He squatted down and ruffled the pup's ears, then gazed at her, his blue eyes full of reassurance. "If that's okay with you?"

No, it wasn't okay with her. It wasn't that she couldn't trust Casey with Ally. He'd raised Audrey from a young age and knew the ropes. If anything, he'd been overprotective of his little sister. It wasn't that. She didn't want to get too chummy with her *new* old next-door neighbor. And she certainly didn't want Ally getting close to him, either.

Ally reached up and put her palms on Susie's cheeks, looking into her eyes. "Pleeeeeze."

The kid knew how to get to her; her plea zigzagged to her heart. She shouldn't deny Ally a small measure of happiness because of pride. Ally had suffered enough sadness for someone so young.

With a shake of her head aimed at Casey, she lowered Ally to the ground. "Okay. You mind what Casey says, sweetie and stay close."

The puppy immediately raced to Ally's feet, his tail circling like a windmill on a breezy day.

They were becoming fast friends.

That wasn't good.

Sighing, Susanna walked to her door, climbed up the steps and swiveled her head. She spotted Ally laughing as the bushy-haired pup did impressive belly rolls on the grass. Casey glanced over and their eyes met. A second ticked by, and then another. Having him here was impossible. She didn't want him watching her. The corners of her lips pulled down and she snapped out of his momentary hold on her. Reaching for the screen door, she turned the handle and stepped inside her home.

Escaping.

Casey leaned against his SUV with his arms folded over his chest, keeping an eye on Ally. The dog was pooped out from one too many belly rolls and Ally sat beside him on the grass, talking up a storm. Casey didn't know two-year-olds could babble so much, yet Charger listened to the blonde girl with ears perked and tongue hanging as if he understood every word she said. Casey knew a little bit about Ally from what Audrey had told him. Mainly that she'd lost her mom, Rhonda Lee, to drug addiction. Rhonda Lee and Susanna were first cousins. Since the child's father was out of the picture, Susanna had been the child's only option and she'd stepped in to raise the little girl.

Susanna's screen door squeaked open and he spotted her stepping off the porch. As she walked toward him, she was ramrod stiff, her shoulders tight, her pretty sculpted chin held high. She hadn't forgiven him. That much was clear.

Ten years seemed like eons ago, but Casey hadn't forgotten the night they'd made love either. He was totally to blame for the awkward situation between them and it made his mission here that much harder. Somehow, he had to gain Susanna's trust so he could help her. He owed the Hart family that much. Without Eleanor and George Hart, he would've never been able to raise Audrey on his own. For years, they'd been her second family when Casey was on the road with the rodeo.

If he hadn't had legitimate business here establishing new Sentinel Construction offices in Reno and overseeing the final stages of a trendy new restaurant on the River Walk, Audrey wouldn't have pounced on the idea of him moving into their childhood home to secretly help Susanna get back on her feet.

"She's all alone, Case. Trying hard to make a success of Sweet Susie's and raise her cousin's child on her own," Audrey had said. "You know how that is."

And he did. He'd had his share of struggles after they'd lost their parents and he'd had to grow up fast in order to raise his much younger sister. That's why he'd allowed Audrey to twist his arm. The trouble with the plan was that Susanna was barely speaking to him.

She glanced at the dog cozying up next to Ally under the shade of a cottonwood tree and then pursed her lips and robotically proceeded toward them. He sighed. She wasn't happy about the pup being here either.

That was another one of Audrey's ideas. Not that Casey minded rescuing the dog from a puppy mill, but he hadn't planned on bringing the dog with him on this trip. He could've left the dog with Audrey at Sunset Ranch, but his sister had insisted he'd need the company. Now, he got it. His shrewd sister meant for the pup to be an icebreaker. Judging by the look on Susie's face, he might also need a chisel.

"Here you go." Susie dangled the key with its cupcake-shaped clear plastic keychain that read SweetSusies.com in bright lavender letters.

Casey opened his palm and she dropped it in, but as he lifted his hand, their fingertips brushed. Susie's eyes widened and she blinked. Touching him made her nervous. That annoyed the crap out of him. Why was that? "I don't bite, Suse."

"No one calls me that anymore."

Meaning she didn't want him calling her by that familiar nickname. He'd heard Audrey refer to Susanna that way since forever. "I'll try to remember that."

He closed his hand over the key. "You've started a business. You always were a damn good cook. How's it going?"

Her gaze slid to Ally. The child was content watching the dog resting beside her. Susanna turned back to Casey and said, "It's going…well. I love what I do and…that's all that matters."

It was the defiant way she said *all that matters* and the way her eyes darted away afterward that caught his attention. Audrey had said she was struggling with all the changes in her life, but Susanna was too darned prideful to ask for help. "I hear you. It's always a good thing," he said, squinting his eyes, his emotions stirring, "to love what you do."

Nervously, she nibbled her lower lip. He'd always thought she was pretty, in a natural wholesome sort of way. If he were any other man, under different circumstances, he'd be damned happy finding out Susanna was going to be his temporary next-door neighbor. Too bad the situation was more complicated than that.

"Oh, I'm….sorry. I shouldn't have said…" She nibbled her lip some more.

"It's okay."

She couldn't hide her compassion, not even under the guise of defiance. But he didn't want anyone's pity. His lifelong dream had been cut short by a freakish fall off a bucking bronco, but he'd come out the other end okay. As a rodeo rider, he'd known the risks. Because of sound investments he'd made during his heyday as a champion, he'd become CEO of Sentinel Construction and was wealthy enough to buy a rodeo or two of his own now. "My rodeo days are behind me. I'm fine with it."

She swallowed and nodded. "Well…I really should take Ally inside. It's almost suppertime."

"Yeah and I'd better get unloaded." He gazed toward the front door of his house. A dozen memories he wasn't expecting flooded his mind. He'd raised Audrey here. It hadn't been easy being mother and father to a sister eight years his junior. The responsibility had weighed heavily on him. Audrey would say he'd been hardnosed and a bully, and more times than not, he'd worried that he'd messed up her life. But the Harts had always been there for her, giving her guidance and a second roof over her head. All the more reason Casey had to see this thing through with Susanna. "It's been years since I've lived here." He sighed, speaking his thoughts aloud.

"It's strange having the house empty since Audrey moved out."

"Yeah, who knows what I'll find in there," he said.

"Except for some dust, you won't be disappointed. Audrey kept the place up."

"I bet you miss her," he said, sliding his gaze to her.

Susanna looked longingly toward the house. "I do, but… she's happy and a new mommy now."

"It appears you're doing some mothering too."

A warm glow entered Susanna's eyes as she continued to gaze at the house. "I'm doing my best with Ally. She's really a sweetheart. Well, like I said, I'd better be going."

"Yeah. Thanks for the key. I'll see you around," he said. "Bye, now."

She turned to walk away. With her long auburn tresses pulled into a ponytail, she looked younger than her twenty-eight years, but the snug fit of her blue jeans and the form-fitted plaid blouse she wore screamed *woman* in capital letters.

His problem wasn't going away. Susanna had refused eye contact for all but a second or two of their awkward conversation, which she couldn't wait to end.

Great.

Walking to the back of his SUV, he pressed the remote button on his keychain. The trunk eased open and he reached inside to retrieve his luggage. Gripping the handles of his leather suitcases with both hands, he gave a yank and hoisted them out.

"Charger," he called over to the lazy dog. The pup's head shot up and he spotted Ally and Susanna climbing the steps of the house. He rose on all fours, gave himself a shake and then trotted toward Susanna's house. "No," Casey commanded.

The pup stopped in his tracks and hung his head. "You can't go over there."

We're not welcome.

Yet.

When the alarm clock went off the next morning, Susanna opened her eyes and glanced at the time. 4:00 a.m. She groaned softly and slid her arm out from under her pillow to hush the grating sound before it woke Ally in her bedroom two doors down. She stretched her arms over her head and yawned. Waking up at this ungodly hour had now become her routine. Rising in the dark was necessary. She had a full morning of baking ahead of her and had to get up an hour earlier than usual to make up for time spent with Ally in the mornings.

She hinged her body up and focused her eyes, going over the to-do list in her head. Aside from the regular orders from local merchants she would hand deliver, she also had to package muffins to send to a few clients in the surrounding counties.

Tossing her sheet off, she bounded quietly from bed and tiptoed out of the room and into the hallway. Wooden floorboards squeaked under her slight weight and she cringed. When Ally had first got here, there'd been too many nights when she woke from bad dreams. Susanna sent up a silent prayer that she'd sleep soundly for a few more hours. She popped her head inside the bedroom and smiled, sighing quietly. Blond curls framed Ally's face as she slept on the twin bed that had once been Susanna's. She never got over the love she felt for the little girl, or how the sight of her peaceful and happy made jelly of her heart.

"Promise me, you'll take her and raise her right," Susanna's drug-addicted cousin would say, "if anything happens to me. The kid deserves a better life."

Susanna had promised and Rhonda Lee had tried to kick her cocaine habit. She'd been to rehab twice, but there was a high failure rate with addicts trying to come clean and Rhonda Lee hadn't made it to her twenty-ninth birthday. With no father in the picture, and all the other relatives too old to take on a young child, Susanna was Ally's only hope and her cousin had known it.

There had never been a question that someone else would take Ally in; Susanna's love for little Ally and Rhonda Lee had her immediately accepting the responsibility of raising the child. The sweet little girl needed someone who would give her unconditional but structured love. Rhonda Lee's losing battle with her personal demons had all been terribly hard on the child and Ally deserved better.

Susanna planned to give Ally a good life.

She left the room and walked into the kitchen. She filled the coffeepot and the smell of the rich grounds got her juices flowing. Then she turned the oven on to preheat. "Don't fail me," she muttered to the late-seventies olive green appliance.

She got out all the bowls, muffin tins, utensils and ingredients she needed and began to bake. She had it timed perfectly—after mixing up and setting two dozen rocky road chocolate muffins in the oven she took twenty minutes to shower, throw on her clothes and dry her hair.

When she got back to the kitchen, she put her Sweet Susie's apron on over her head and tied it behind her back. She was right on schedule and after the timer pinged, she donned oven mitts and pulled out the first two dozen muffins, setting the pans to cool on racks. Her next creation was made with cranberries and cheese. The coffeecake-like muffin wasn't too sweet and a favorite at three local coffeehouses where she made deliveries. Once she set them to bake, she dipped her finger into the mixing bowl for a taste test. "Yum."

By the time six-thirty rolled around, she'd baked twelve dozen pastries. Cupcakes and muffins cooled on the counters and tabletops all over the house. Bowls and utensils filled the sink and dots of batter littered the linoleum floor. She stepped carefully. Cleanup didn't come until after she made her deliveries. She sipped from her coffee mug and began placing the pastries inside a Sweet Susie's cake box.

Barking sounds rang out on the quiet street. She knew that bark. Susie moved to the kitchen bay window and gazed out. Charger and his owner jogged by. On short stubbly legs, the puppy was trying his darnedest to keep up with Casey's long purposeful strides. It was no match. The pup's five-foot leash was stretched to its limit. Casey finally slowed to a walk, allowing the puppy time to catch his breath.

Susanna caught her own breath. Casey was dressed in a sleeveless tank top and jogging pants. Golden brown and muscled like a pro athlete, he wasn't hard on the eyes. Her friend Mindy would call him eye candy. With dark blond locks tied back and his skin moist and glistening, he strode confidently along the sidewalk as he cooled down.

She stood immobilized, fascinated by Casey Thomas. What else was new?

When he reached the front of his house, Susie was ready to turn back to her work. But he stopped and angled his head toward her kitchen window. Deep baby blues zeroed in on her, meeting her unflinching stare. Geesh! She didn't have the nerve or good sense to turn away. He grinned and waved, mouthing "Good morning." His smile did ridiculous things to her. A knot formed in her throat and she swallowed past it to wiggle her fingers his way.

She stepped away from the window, reminding herself she had a business to run. She couldn't go around lusting after Casey, of all men. Or losing sleep over him.

After putting the finishing touches on her pastries, she entered Ally's bedroom. She was just waking and Susie whispered, "Good morning, Muffin. Time to get up. We have deliveries to make." Susanna bent to kiss her forehead and ruffle her curls.

Ally darted her gaze around the room and in those first few seconds, curious fear entered her eyes, before she realized where she was. One day she'd wake up and not have to remind herself that her mother was gone, and that her life would never be the same. Susanna prayed that day would come soon. Ally was young enough to acclimate to new surroundings. Susanna had met with a psychologist before taking Ally in and learned that a regular routine and stability were the keys in her acceptance of the situation. She needed no more surprises or traumatic experiences in her young life. She had to feel secure.

"Ready to get dressed? I saved two vanilla cupcakes for you. I have lots and lots of frosting leftover too. Would you like to frost them?"

Ally's eyes widened and she smiled, pushing her covers off and hopefully the sad memories, too. "What flavors?"

"You have a choice of cherry chip or chocolate marshmallow."

"Chocolate marshmallow!"

"Okay, then. Chocolate marshmallow it is."

Susanna hoisted Ally off the bed and set her down. The little girl wiggled herself out of her nightdress and Susanna helped her get her arms through the sleeves of a purple and white Sweet Susie's logo T-shirt. Jeans came on next and then socks. Ally slipped her feet into well-worn hot pink Velcro tennis shoes all by herself. "Good girl. We're almost all set. Let's go wash your face and hands and comb your hair. Then we'll have breakfast and do some frosting." Ally raced to the bathroom and after she was cleaned up, they went to the kitchen.

Shortly after breakfast, a light knocking on the front door disrupted Susanna's muffin count for the last box. She slid a glance out the kitchen window and wrinkled her nose. "Casey," she muttered.

Darn. She had to open the door. He knew she was home. She kept her curtains open to let in early morning sunshine and anyone who was looking could see her bustling about the kitchen.

Sliding her palms down her apron and straightening her ponytail, she made her way to the entrance. "I'll answer the door, sweetie," she said to Ally, who was busy licking chocolate marshmallow frosting off her fingers. "Not too much now. Just one bite of the cupcake." Her mothering skills needed polishing, but at least Ally finished all of her oatmeal this morning before she got her treat.

Susanna took a deep breath, and then gave the door a gentle yank. She came face-to-face with Casey.

"Mornin'," he said, his gaze instantly darting to the lettering on her apron. Sweet Susie's…Tasty Pastries and More.

"Hello." Clean-shaven this morning, his hair combed back, his eyes the deepest azure blue she'd ever seen, he wore a seriously gorgeous beige Armani suit. Wow. He hardly looked like the rough and tumble rodeo rider she'd grown up with. He gestured with his index finger. "What's the more?"

"The more? Oh, on the apron? I do cakes and all kinds of desserts, really."

"Keeping your options open?"

"Yes, I suppose…it makes good business sense."

"But your specialty is muffins and cupcakes?"

"That's right."

"I can smell your baking from my house." He lifted his nose and took a whiff. "Smells amazing, Susanna."

"Thank you. I…uh, would you like a muffin or two?" If only her mother hadn't drilled good manners into her. Last night, she'd felt like a heel seeing him come home with a bag of take-out from Burgers-N-Stuff. They weren't the best burgers in town. Because he was Audrey's brother, and for no other reason, she should have offered to bring him supper on his first night back in town. She glanced at her watch. She was fine on time. "I have to load up soon to make my deliveries but you're welcome to come in for a few minutes."

Say no. Say you have urgent business and you have to be on your way.

"Love to."

Bummer.

He reached for the screen door and Susanna turned around and began walking. "The kitchen's a big mess right now. I clean up after I make deliveries."

As they entered the kitchen, Ally saw Casey and she came forward, peering curiously at him.

"Hi, Ally," he said, bending to her level and softening his voice. "Hey, I like your shirt. Do you help Aunt Susie with baking?"

She nodded. "I frosteded two cupcakes."

"That's real nice." Casey pointed to the tip of her freckled nose. "Did you frost your nose, too?"

She giggled. "No."

"Not on purpose," Susie said.

Ally wiped her nose and removed the frosting. Her mouth turned down. "Where's Charger?"

"Oh, Charger's at my house right now. He's doing just fine, taking a nap."

"Well deserved," Susanna said. "You ran him for all he was worth."

"Yeah, about that." Casey rose to face her. "It's part of the reason I came by."

Her eyes shifted away from his direct look and she turned to the cabinet to grab a plate. *Keep busy, Susie, and keep pretending nothing happened between the two of you.* "It is?"

"I go jogging just about every morning. It didn't occur to me that Charger would make such a darn racket in the neighborhood. He didn't wake Ally up, did he?"

"No, I don't think so. She slept well past the time I... looked out my window and saw you."

He sighed with relief. "Okay, that's good to hear."

She placed one of each kind of muffin she'd baked this morning on a plate and gestured toward the table. "Would you like to have a quick cup of coffee with a muffin?"

"No thanks," he said, sliding into a chair that faced her messy sink and the chipped tiles on the counter. This kitchen, as well as the rest of the house, was a far cry from the luxury Casey was accustomed to now. Audrey had told her he'd invested in a construction company years ago and after the owner retired, Casey became the new CEO. "I don't want to hold you up. I'll just have one of these." He grabbed for the cranberry cheese muffin, took a big bite and chewed thoughtfully. "This is really good."

"Thanks." She picked up a raspberry-filled lemon cupcake and set it in a cake box. She was about to say he'd just ruined the calorie burn from his jog, but guys didn't worry about things like that—not the way women did—and she didn't want to sound snarky.

She closed the box and sealed it with Scotch Tape.

Casey grabbed another muffin and starting chewing again. "Mmm. What's this one called?"

"That's my Sweet and Sassy Caramel-Apple muffin." When she'd tested out the muffin, she'd refined it to make the apple a little tart. Sweet and Sassy had become a best seller. Her small business needed to provide something a little different in order to survive. Competition was fierce and Susie was learning the ropes one secret ingredient at a time.

"It's delicious."

"Thank you." Was there anything more awkward than having Casey sitting in her kitchen taste-testing her pastries? It was a good thing she had to leave soon and their time together would be cut short.

"So you make deliveries every day?"

"Yes, except on Sunday. I cater to the local coffeehouses

and some offices. I do…just about anything that comes up. Parties, birthdays, reunions, anything I can."

"Must be hard getting it all done."

A chuckle blurted from her lips. "You just have to look around this place to see how well I'm doing."

Casey blinked and his expression softened. He didn't bother to glance around her messy kitchen counters.

Oh, boy, she hadn't meant to say that. No one knew how she plotted out every second of every day and still didn't have enough time to do it all. She wasn't one to complain. She certainly didn't want his sympathy. He just made her so darned nervous. Without giving him the chance to offer an obligatory polite answer, she asked, "Did you have something else you wanted? When you came over, I got the impression you—"

"What time does Ally go to sleep?"

Where did that question come from? Was he worried about Charger's barking again? It couldn't be anything else, could it? Blood pounded through her veins and she took a beat to answer. "Eight-ish…why?"

"I'd like to talk to you tonight, after Ally goes to bed."

No. No. No. She put her head down, staring at a drop of creamy batter on the floor. "I usually call Mom after Ally goes to bed."

"It's important," he added.

She didn't want to be alone with him ever again, especially not at night, without Ally as her shield. She had to be up early. She had a headache. She had a friend coming over. Half a dozen other pitiful phony excuses entered her mind.

Finally, she lifted her lids and met his gaze. His blue eyes bored into her in a breathtaking way and all of his charming sincerity hit home. *Oh, man.* She couldn't wiggle out of this without looking like a liar. Except for calling her mom to check in and say hello, she had no plans tonight. It was the same old, same old. She sighed. "Okay."

On a solid nod, he rose from his seat and pointed to the boxes. "Where do these go?"

"In my minivan."

"I'll help load them."

"No, it's not necessary…. Don't you have to be somewhere?" she asked. He was dressed to kill. He must have a zillion more important things to do than load up her cupcakes and muffins.

He shrugged and carefully lifted a box in his arms. "Let me worry about that. Is your van in the garage?"

"Yes, uh, thanks."

He headed toward the door leading to the garage.

With Ally beside her, she grabbed a box and followed him. The garage smelled musty and contained the heat of summery days. It was dark inside until she pressed the garage door opener. Daylight poured through and she squinted as she walked to the end of the van. Balancing a box in one hand she opened the back hatch with the other.

Casey peered inside the van. "Nice set up," he said. "Did you buy it this way?"

"No. It was converted for me."

When she didn't say more, Casey probed, "Your boyfriend do it for you?"

She pursed her lips. Heavens, she didn't have time for a boyfriend. Dating was a thing of the past. "My mother."

She guided her box onto one of the metal shelves and Casey did the same with his. His elbow brushed the slope of her breast where her Sweet Susie's apron met her blouse. Her breath came up short, but she continued on, trying to ignore the warm buzz rippling through her.

"Mom gave me the van on *her* wedding day. She had the back converted with shelves for my cake boxes and then commissioned a designer to paint my logo on the sides of the van."

It was a ten-year-old minivan, all that her mother had

apologetically said she could afford, but it was in good enough shape for her purposes. Her mom really splurged on the logo design and on the day of her second wedding to Chip Huffman, a man who loved her to distraction, she'd taken Susanna outside, to show her the van. "Accepting this is the best wedding gift you could ever give me. I think your dad would think so too," she'd said to Susanna.

There was no way to deny her mother the pleasure. Her mom had seen her struggle to get her pastries to customers by stuffing her cake boxes in the trunk and backseat of her beat-up sedan. Often, Susanna would pray to the pothole gods and drive as slowly as eighty-five-year-old Mrs. Simpson from five houses down to deliver her pastries in one piece. Eleanor Hart had skimped on her own wedding just to be able to surprise Susanna with the gift. Susanna had been so grateful and overwhelmed, she'd cried for five full minutes.

"Your mom is a special lady," Casey said, his smile easy.

Well that was something they both agreed on. Her mother had tended to her dad for years, pretending his declining health hadn't taken a toll on her as well. But Susanna knew what it had cost her mother. Several years ago, her mom met Chip Huffman through a mutual friend and she'd fallen in love with the Georgia peach grower. Susanna had encouraged the relationship—her mom deserved some happiness in the second half of her life. And now, her mother was living in Georgia, soon to celebrate her third wedding anniversary.

"She is…thank you."

After that, they worked like a team to get the rest of the boxes loaded, Casey refusing to take no for an answer. He waited while Susanna buckled Ally into her car seat and hoisted herself into the driver seat. As she backed out of the garage, he followed her on foot along the driveway.

The garage door closed behind him and he waved. "I'll see you tonight."

Shoot. For a minute, she'd forgotten about that.

Her fingers dug into the steering wheel and she sighed as the van ambled down the street.

One thing was certain: Casey Thomas wasn't coming over tonight to talk about the dog.

Two

"Morning, Susie and Ally," Miranda Fillmore's voice boomed as she walked out the back door of The Coffee Connection. Dressed in a chocolate-brown apron, the forty-something coffeehouse manager greeted them with her usual cheerful smile.

Ally waved to her from the car seat. "Hi!"

"Good morning, Miranda," Susanna said, bounding out of the minivan. She had to make five deliveries this morning, all before eight o'clock, so she'd learned how to work fast.

Miranda hid something behind her back as she approached Susanna. Away from Ally's line of vision, she whipped a bright pink coloring book and a new box of crayons under Susanna's nose. "Can she have these?" she whispered.

"Oh, of course." Three fairy-tale princesses wearing tiaras and frilly gowns adorned the coloring book cover. "She loves anything with princesses."

Susanna appreciated Miranda asking about giving her the gift. Being new to mothering, Susanna made daily decisions for Ally she wasn't used to making. Most of them seemed like common sense, but she'd still gone online and read books, researching child rearing tips and techniques regardless. She didn't want to slip up and do something wrong when it came to Ally.

"I thought so." Miranda said. "What little girl wouldn't? I was hoping it would brighten her day."

"Spreading a little joy is always a good thing."

Miranda walked to Ally's side of the minivan and opened the door. "Here you go, Ally. These are for you. I hope you like to color."

The little girl's eyes lit up as she reached out to claim the unexpected gift. "Princesses!" She hugged the book to her chest, and then studied the slender new box of washable—*thank you, Miranda*—crayons.

Susanna's heart warmed. Since Ally had come to live with her, her clients had been overly accommodating by allowing her a little later delivery time and sending someone out to help her unload the boxes. All of them seemed to understand the plight of a working single mother, and were very kind and attentive to Ally. "What do you say, Ally?"

"Thank you!"

"It's very sweet of you, Miranda," Susanna said.

"You're both very welcome." Miranda walked over to her. "But what's sweet are these lovelies." She reached for the box with The Coffee Connection written on top. "What did you bring me today?"

"The usual assortment of two dozen muffins and the cupcake of the day, which is peanut butter with chocolate ganache frosting."

"Yummy. Those will go by lunchtime," Miranda said. "I hope you brought me a dozen of those?"

"I sure did. Well, I'm off. Thanks again for thinking of Ally. She'll be coloring all afternoon, I'm sure."

"You're welcome. Bye now."

Susanna drove off. After she made the rest of her deliveries, she steered the minivan toward home. She didn't mind being up and out early, but she felt bad for disrupting

Ally's sleep every morning. Once she opened her own shop, her traipsing around town in Sweet Susie's minivan would come to an end. For a moment, she let herself daydream about the lavender and white painted shop, its bakery cases filled with dozens upon dozens of her pastries. There would be café tables and chairs under a giant blackboard chalked with the day's cupcake specials. She'd have two employees and a delivery man. Everyone would wear lavender.

Sure, Susie...keep dreaming.

She sighed quietly.

Ally would be going to kindergarten in two years and she'd have more time to build her business. If she could hold on until then....

A few minutes later, she pulled up to the house and drove into the garage. Ally had fallen asleep. Susanna took her time working on the straps to ease Ally out of the car seat. Ally opened her eyes once, draped her arms around Susanna's neck and curled her body against hers, snuggling in. Susanna kissed the top of her head as she made her way into the house. In the bedroom, she lowered Ally down onto her bed. The child nestled her face into her pillow and Susanna tiptoed out of the room.

In the kitchen, Susanna filled the sink with detergent and rinsed her bowls, muffin tins and utensils, giving each one a good scrub. She had an ancient dishwasher that would go on the fritz every so often, but today she was an optimist. She loaded it up, hit the sanitize button and closed the door. "Do your magic," she said and walked away to clean countertops and pretend she didn't notice the peeling paint on the walls and the permanently scuffed floors. The house really needed a makeover, but Susanna would be happy with a brand spanking new double stainless steel oven that would bake four dozen anything in one shot—one with even heat distribution that turned into a convection oven with the press of a button.

Susanna walked into Ally's room and stole a peek to make sure she was still asleep, then retrieved her laptop and set it up on the kitchen table. When her cell phone rang and the caller's name popped up, she smiled and answered. "You just saved me."

"From dishes or from doing the books?" her friend Mindy asked.

"The books."

"Well, you can thank me later. How's Ally?"

"She's doing okay. Taking a little nap right now."

"Give her a hug for me when she wakes up."

"I'll do that."

"So I need the scoop. Did he show up?"

"He?"

"You know who I mean. My junior high school fantasy crush. Casey. Is he really back in town?"

Susanna's face scrunched up. She'd almost forgotten Mindy's fascination with Casey Thomas when they were growing up. She and Mindy had been friendly as young-sters, but not besties, the way she and Audrey were. But their friendship had developed once they were adults. "Yes, as of yesterday. How'd you find out so fast?"

"I bumped into Lana Robards at the market this morn-ing. She said she saw Casey jogging in the neighborhood." Mindy's hearty laughter bubbled through the cell phone. "She said he was enough incentive to take up running again."

"She just got divorced," Susanna blurted. Something painful knifed through her stomach. She didn't want to think about why hearing that bothered her so much.

"Not just. It's been a year. And it must be lonely for her on the weeks she doesn't have her kids."

Darlene and Darryl were four-year-old twins living with one parent one week and one parent the next under the terms of their joint custody agreement. It was tough and Susanna often wondered how the children were adjusting.

"But I digress. So tell me your impressions. Is he still dreamy?"

"Are you forgetting about Ted, your loyal, wonderful hubby, or that you're six months prego?"

"C'mon Susie, give me something to spice up my ho-hum life. I'm a grade school teacher with summer-itis. Since school let out, I miss my students and my work. And Ted's been smothering me with kindness."

"You love every second of it. You don't fool me."

"So," she whispered. "Just tell me, is Casey still hot?"

Susanna rolled her eyes. "Yes, okay. Casey is still good-looking." Mindy would have melted into a puddle of drool today if she'd seen him dressed in that gunmetal gray tailored Armani suit. "He's a little more solid, not as lean as in his bronc-busting days."

"Mmm. Solid is good. Have you spoken to him?"

She so did not want to have this conversation. "A little."

"And, what's the scoop? Why's he here? How long will he be staying next door?"

Being a teacher, Mindy had to know all the facts. "All I know is that he's here on business. I have no clue how long he's staying."

But he'll be coming over to my house tonight after Ally goes to sleep. Her eyes squeezed shut and she rubbed the left side of her temple. She had hours before she had to think about that.

"But not permanently?"

"No." Audrey had assured her this was only temporary... and the more temporary the better.

"Oh, Susie...you've got to work on your spice skills. You didn't give me anything juicy."

"I'll remember that in the future."

"Hey, I almost forgot the real reason I called. One of

the teachers I work with is throwing her daughter a sweet sixteen party. I told her about Sweet Susie's and how fabulous your desserts are. She's going to call you later today to cater a chocolate party for her."

"Wow, thanks. That sounds like fun. I can certainly use the extra work."

"Welcome. Oh, and Suse…it wouldn't hurt if you invited Casey over for dinner one night. He's single, you're single. Who knows?"

"Oh, no. Don't even go there, Mindy. You're not matchmaking for me. The last date I went on was a disaster and lasted all of forty-five minutes before I showed him the door."

"That wasn't my fault. I didn't know the guy I set you up with was a-a…."

"I'll say it. He was a grabby-handed sex addict."

"I've apologized for that a dozen times. Besides, it would be different with Casey. You know him."

Too well. He'd broken her heart once already. She didn't want an encore performance. "Not interested."

Mindy sighed melodramatically. "Most single women would jump at the chance to date a hot guy like Casey, but my friend only gets her jollies from a *hot* oven."

Mindy was darn right. And that's exactly how it was going to stay.

Casey thought after taming wild broncos half his life, he'd be used to confrontation. But the idea of speaking with Susanna about the sins of the past left a bitter taste in his mouth. Taking his little sister's vulnerable friend in the living room of his home hadn't been one of his proudest moments. The guilt weighed heavily on him. They'd never spoken of it. Susanna probably wanted to forget it had ever happened. How could he blame her? That night, Susie had come to his house looking for Audrey and some comfort.

She'd been devastated learning of her father's debilitating disease, knowing his life would be changed forever and death wasn't far in his future. But she'd found Casey instead, and he'd taken her virginity. Tonight, he had to right the wrong. There was no doubt in his mind.

"Has to be done," he said, his voice breaking the silence. The pup's head shot up from his sprawled position on the bedroom floor. His tail wiggled and he rose to stretch his neck. His round chestnut eyes zeroed in on Casey. "Hey, I wish I could take you over there tonight, but I can't count on that yapper of yours not going off."

Charger's head tilted.

"Don't give me that pathetic look. You're staying."

The pup hung his head, walked around in a circle a few times and settled into another sprawl right beside the bed.

Casey smiled. Audrey had been right about one thing: Charger was good company. The grateful pup had greeted him as if he was something special when Casey walked through the front door today. After a long day of meetings, the pup was a welcome sight. Playing with Charger for half an hour in the backyard got his mind off work and off his last meeting of the day…with Susanna.

He tucked his blue plaid shirt into well-worn Wrangler jeans and buckled his belt. A glance in the mirror told him he'd need a haircut soon, but just a trim. He liked the longer style. Call it rebellion from his old rodeo days. There were still traces of the old unbroken Casey in him and he didn't ever want to lose that part of himself.

He glanced at his wristwatch. Eight-thirty. "Okay, here goes," he said. "Be good, pup."

Halfway out the front door, he stopped short, turned and walked into the kitchen. Opening the refrigerator, he stared at the contents. He had to get some food stocked; the fridge was downright depressing. He grabbed two cold beers and shouldered the door shut. "What the heck."

He didn't know if Susanna liked beer. He didn't know much about her at all, really. Not Susanna, the adult. On a deep breath and holding the beers as a peace offering, he exited the house and walked the short distance to his neighbor's house. Rapping his knuckles lightly on the screen door, he waited.

It took a minute for her to open the door. She stood behind the mesh screen, her eyes focused somewhere between his neck and shoulders. "Hi." He kept his voice low. "Is Ally sleeping?"

"Yes, I just finished reading to her and she's out."

He smiled to himself as the image flashed of Susie sitting next to Ally on her bed, getting cozy and snuggling together. He gestured to the porch. "It's a nice night. Wanna sit out on the steps?"

Her gaze flew toward the hallway and she listened for a second. "Okay. If I keep the door open, I can listen for Ally in case she wakes up."

"Sounds like a plan."

She stepped outside, and quietly closed the screen door. Casey waited for her take a seat. Of course, she hugged the farthest side of the porch steps. Casey took his cue and sat on the opposite end. Three feet separated them. It probably hurt her shoulders to sit so stiffly. She hugged her arms around her middle and focused her attention on the sky, a slice of the moon, the large cottonwood by the sidewalk. Anywhere but at him. "Would you like one?" he asked, lifting a beer her way.

"Oh, uh," she glanced at the bottle. "Sure."

She reached for it and his finger brushed hers as they made the exchange. Casey met her eyes in that moment and she shifted her gaze to the ground. "How was your day?" he asked.

"Busy, but good."

"Get all your deliveries made?"

"Yeah, I did. Worked on the books and made a few more batches of muffins and cupcakes this afternoon."

"For?"

"I have online orders too. I package them up and send them locally to three other counties. There's just a handful of customers right now but I'm hoping to…" She shrugged. "Never mind."

"You're hoping to expand?" Casey guessed. She was passionate about what she did. Her nerves and whatever anger she held toward him couldn't disguise her excitement.

"Open my own shop one day." She raised the beer bottle to her lips and took a big gulp.

He nodded and took a swig too. "I remember you liked cooking. You were always helping your mother in the kitchen, but how did you get into this business?"

"I fell into it really. When Dad's multiple sclerosis got real bad, I quit college and came back home to help my mother care for him. My mom was working part-time back then and she just couldn't do it all. I could see the strain on her face and it was getting worse every day. My dad had good days and bad days. MS is like that. Every day was a new experience. On the good days, we'd do whatever he felt like doing, playing checkers, watching movies, occasionally we'd go on an outing. On the bad days, when all he could do was stay in bed, I'd dabble in the kitchen and come up with recipes for cupcakes. When visitors stopped by, I'd offer them one of my creations. Everyone seemed to love them and they began asking me to bake for their children's birthday parties or special occasions. After Dad died, I—I—uh, sorry," she choked out.

Her eyes clouded up with tears and she didn't finish her sentence. One tear fell onto her cheek. *Oh, man.* Why'd he have to ask her about her business? Audrey had already filled him on some of her story. But was it a sin to try to get her to speak to him? Or even look him straight in the eye? Protective urges warred inside his acid-drenched gut. It was all he could do to keep from reaching for her to give her the comfort she needed.

To help make the sadness go away.

He knew the pain of losing a parent. When he was a teenager, a deadly storm had taken the lives of both of his folks. The ache never fully went away. It was there and sometimes a random memory would come out of nowhere and shatter him.

"Are you okay?" he asked.

She straightened and pulled herself together, using the back of her hand to wipe moisture from her eyes. "I will be. I...I don't usually do this. It's just that...sometimes it hits me all over again."

"I know the feeling."

A sigh wobbled from her lips. "I know you do."

Keep her talking. "Audrey told me after George died, you continued living here to help your mother adjust."

"Yeah, I did." Susanna leaned forward, braced her elbows on her knees and cradled her face with her palms. Gazing straight ahead, she went on, "Mom was a mess. She needed me, so I stayed, but I had to earn a living. We'd been scraping by and we really needed the money. That's when Sweet Susie's was born."

"You put your life on hold for your dad and mom."

She shrugged. "I wanted to do it. To me, there was no other option."

She wasn't his sister's silly young friend anymore. Her loyalty and dedication to her family was admirable...and rare. Just when she had an opportunity to branch out on her own, she'd taken Ally in because the child had nowhere else to go, as Audrey had put it.

If only he wasn't noticing how Susanna Hart had grown into a pretty sensational woman all around.

He studied her profile. Her chin was delicate, her cheekbones high, her skin dewy soft. Her ponytail hung loose. Long wispy strands of hair framed her face, the color reminding him of autumn leaves right before they turned, golden in some spots, red in others, blending naturally into something phenomenal.

His gaze dipped to her soft shoulders exposed by the cotton tank top she wore and then farther down to where her top dipped into a smooth valley covering her breasts, which were round and amazingly full for her small stature. She had to be five-foot-four to his six-foot-two. Because he was a glutton for punishment he gave her legs a quick once over. She was wearing shorts. It wasn't her fault it was summer and she had long, gorgeous, tanned legs. He tried his damnedest not to stare at them.

Ten years ago, those legs had wrapped around him. She'd fit him perfectly and it hadn't been awkward making love to her. No, the awkwardness had come immediately afterward, once he'd realized what he'd done.

Crap. He had no business going there. No business stirring up trouble in his head.

He took a swallow of his beer and pulled his gaze away, looking out at the same aggravating tree she'd been focused on since she stepped out of her house.

No one said another word.

Casey sipped his beer quietly and put his thirty-five-year-old hormones on notice. He'd be damned not to say what he'd come here to say to Susanna. His mission was clear. First he needed to break the ice and gain her friendship back. He saw no way around it.

He set his bottle down, stretched out one leg and pivoted his body toward her. "We should probably talk about it, Susanna," he said quietly.

Her eyes squeezed shut. She made no effort to conceal her dismay and when she opened them again, that damned tree still held her attention. "I don't think it's necessary."

"I do."

"Why? It's in the past."

"Because we're neighbors again and you haven't looked me in the eye since I got here."

"Have too."

"Not for more than a second and only when you had no other choice."

Her mouth twisted and she turned sharply, forcing her eyes to his. "I'm looking at you now."

He nodded. "That's a start."

"A start?" she asked.

Her heart beat wildly in her chest, her pulse pounding in her ears. Casey had no idea what he'd done to her that night. Or how hard it was for her to face the man she'd wanted for so long. That night, he hadn't *taken* her virginity. She'd offered it to him without words, but with every emotion she'd held inside. She'd wanted him to be her first. She'd needed his comfort and his body and hadn't felt an iota of guilt about what she'd done.

But she'd had no idea that he would rebuke her so harshly right afterward. She had no idea how many years the hurt would linger.

"We were friends once," he said.

Her eyes begged to narrow, her lips warred to tighten but amazingly she kept composed. "You want us to be friends again?"

There was a long pause before he nodded. "Yeah."

Why had he hesitated? This meeting had been all his idea. Was he allowing the idea to sink in with her? Or was it something else?

"Is it because Audrey and I are friends?"

He gave that some thought. "Partly, but mostly it's because you ran out that night and we…I've always felt badly about the way things ended up between us. When you came looking for Audrey that night, I saw how upset you were. All I wanted to do was comfort you in Audrey's absence. I wanted to help. I never thought it would lead to…to—"

"I get it, Casey. You gave me pity sex."

"Crap, Suse," he shot back as if she'd set him on fire. "I didn't say that."

His eyes darkened, but she didn't back down. He didn't intimidate her. He wanted this conversation and now he was going to get it. "You thought you took advantage of me? You feel guilty as hell about it, don't you?"

"Hell, yeah…I do. I called you that night to apologize. To make sure you were okay."

Susanna took a deep breath. "I wasn't okay."

Casey shut his eyes and rubbed at his temples. "Oh, man…I know."

"You don't know, Casey. You haven't got a clue."

"I know I hurt you…I spoke harshly to you afterwards. I was mad at myself more than anything and everything I said to you that night came out wrong."

"You got that part right."

"I should've known better. I mean, you and I…we weren't anything but—"

"But what?" A short gasp escaped her throat. "We were never really friends. I was your little sister's good buddy and you mostly tolerated me."

"Not true. I liked you. Those last few years, we hung out. You, me and Audrey."

"You treated your sister like a baby and so you thought of me in the same way."

"I know I was hard on Audrey. I tried to raise her right, but what the hell did I know about raising a kid? A girl, no less. She was so much younger than me and I felt I had to protect her, even if I did bully her sometimes."

"I was eighteen when we were together, Casey. I wasn't a kid. I didn't need your protection. I knew what I wanted."

"You didn't want me....You came over looking for Audrey. She would've made you feel better about your dad. She would've had the right words for you. What I did wasn't right. There's no way to take it back, but I've been sorry ever since."

A fiery spear singed her heart and burned its way through her body. She fought to keep from sagging. Her throat thickened, his words of regret ringing in her ears.

He'd been sorry about laying her down on the sofa, comforting her with kisses that healed her open wounds? He'd been sorry about his whispered words that brought her joy and then he'd been sorry about joining their bodies...in a gentle and beautiful way that had made her forget her heartache? Making love with him had been a magical, wonderful experience in her life. She'd been infatuated with her neighbor since age fifteen and had dreamt about being in his arms, having his lips on her and giving her body to him.

For Casey, it had all been one gigantic mistake.

Images from ten years ago seared her memory.

Susanna remembered the shattering sound that had filled her ears that night. She'd rushed into the kitchen. A ceramic mug lay shattered in pieces on the floor. Luckily, there hadn't been steaming coffee bubbling out of it like the last time her dad had a clumsy spill. George Hart stood in the middle of the mess and his bewildered stare hit home. He hadn't been himself lately. Her mom's gaze stayed on her dad and he gently nodded to her. Then her mother asked Susie to sit down. There was something important she needed to know.

"Dad's had the condition for two years, honey, but we felt you didn't have to know. We tried to spare you some worry. But it's time now to tell you the total truth."

Susanna's whole world had crumbled. Now she understood their motives for holding back the truth, but back then she'd been devastated that her father's death was imminent and that both her parents had lied to her about it. Their betrayal had struck deep and she was angry at them, angry at the world. She'd marched defiantly out of the house, but the second she stepped outside, she broke down and sobbed and sobbed.

"You don't have be sorry anymore, Case. Or feel guilty."

A wince drew his mouth down and his eyes filled with grief. "That's not easy to do, Susanna."

"It'll be easier when I tell you the truth. That night, I knew Audrey wasn't home. She was volunteering at the animal hospital and they'd needed someone to stay until midnight. I didn't come to your house looking for Audrey, Casey. I knew she wouldn't be there."

Casey leaned way back and blinked. "What are you saying?"

She stopped short. His sharp question had her doubting herself. But she'd gone this far. He needed to know the truth. Her chin up, she pressed on. "What I'm saying is I knew you'd be there alone. I came for you. You just assumed I was looking for Audrey."

He began shaking his head as if absorbing what she'd just revealed. Well, hell…he'd brought the subject up. Now, he wasn't happy with the truth?

A car cruised down the street and briefly shined light on her house as it passed by. They both watched the driver turn into a driveway at the end of the block.

Casey sighed.

"So you see, you didn't take advantage of me. I came looking for comfort."

"Don't try to make me feel better about this, Susanna. My comforting got outta control."

"I didn't see it that way," she whispered.

Casey sighed again. "I just made things worse. You ran away crying. And things have been weird between us ever since."

"It was an emotional night for me." She'd been crazy about him and the instant he'd touched her, she'd been ready for more. She'd wanted him—the forbidden, brooding rodeo rider—for years. Maybe it was just infatuation but at the time she'd thought it was love, and he'd made her gloriously happy that night. For that brief bit of time, she'd forgotten about her father's illness and the dread that had crawled up inside her.

"I'm sorry about it, Susanna," Casey said in a low rasp. "I didn't mean to hurt you."

She bobbed her head up and down. He'd humiliated and rejected her. The searing ache had festered inside of her for years. Maybe too many years. Could she be using Casey, breaker of her heart, as a scapegoat for her real loss? Had it been the idea of losing her father, not Casey's behavior, that had really devastated her? Was it time to let Casey off the hook? Maybe he was right in confronting her and making them talk it out. He had a point. They were going to be neighbors again. How on earth could she keep Ally from the adorable pup next door? All day long, the little girl had begged to see Charger again.

Susanna's breath caught whenever she looked at Casey, but she could control that, couldn't she? He wasn't *that* irresistible. Having this talk cleared the air. Accepting what was done was done would make life so much less complicated since Casey was her best friend's brother.

"Okay. I accept your apology. What happened between us was a long time ago. I've almost forgotten about it," she lied.

His brows lifted and he smiled. "That's what I was hoping for."

A gnawing ache pinched her belly. His enthusiasm wasn't easy to take. She would forever hold dear the first time she'd made love to a man…a special man whom she might very well have loved. Those memories would never leave her.

"Then we can move on? Start fresh?" he asked.

"I think so."

But she would've been happier if he'd never come back to town.

Three

Susanna put two dozen double chocolate muffins in the oven, set the egg timer and then spread her palms over her apron, smoothing it out. One more batch to go and she'd be done this morning. She strode to the kitchen window and gazed out at the sun-soaked street. A scorcher, the weathercaster had warned. She didn't doubt it. Beads of moisture already trickled down her neck. It was going to be a steam-rising-from-asphalt kind of day.

She spotted a tall figure running up the street. Instead of backing away from the window, she strained to focus on Casey doing his daily exercise. His strides were long and efficient and smooth. She sighed. Why was she punishing herself by searching for him?

As he approached the house, she took a few steps back, out of view of her window. Good. His run was over. He'd go inside his house now and let her get on with her day.

Then she heard footfalls on her driveway, quickly followed by a light rapping on her door. It had to be Casey. He was the only person on the street as of three seconds ago. Apparently, starting fresh *started* early for Casey. "Darn it," she muttered.

Last night they'd parted as "friends." What on earth did he want now?

She opened the door. He stood on her doorstep, hands on hips, chest heaving up and down, wearing black nylon running shorts and a round-necked T-shirt. A headband kept blond locks from falling onto his face, which was coated in a sheen of sweat. He put up a finger, silently asking her to wait until he caught his breath. The dog was nowhere in sight.

Seconds ticked by. He filled her doorway and she stared at him. How could she not? He looked heaven sent standing on her threshold, neck bulging, shoulders broad and muscles tight. Her pulse raced. She'd bet her heart was beating faster than his, and her only exercise this morning had been to lift muffin tins out of the oven.

"Morning," he said at last.

"Good morning. Where's Charger today?"

"I figured I wouldn't punish him. I needed a fast run today. But some days I have to go slower."

She nodded. She got it. His back had never been the same since his injury.

"Is Ally still sleeping?"

"Yes. I'll be getting her up in a few minutes."

His gaze lifted to her hair, hanging loosely past her shoulders. Darned hairclips weren't worth their weight in chocolate chips. They'd fallen out while she was working on batter and she'd forgotten to tie her hair back up.

"I'd ask you in, but…"

"No problem. I had a thought and wanted to run it by you. Any chance you can bake up some of those amazing muffins for my crew?"

"Your crew?"

"Yeah, at the restaurant. I spoke to the foreman yesterday. The guys are busting their asses, working day and night to finish the project on time. Your muffins will take the frowns off their faces in the morning."

"How many are we talking about?"

"Three dozen a day would work."

"Every day?" She did some mental calculations. She could use the extra money.

"Yes, until the restaurant is ready to open. The construction is going on at the River Walk. You could make it your last stop of the morning. Doesn't matter what time they get delivered."

"Oh, uh…sure. I'd love to."

"Wanna start tomorrow?"

She gave it less than one second of thought. "Yes, I can manage that."

"That's great. I'll get the info to you later today. Gotta take a shower now."

"O-kay." Instantly, she pictured him stripping off his workout clothes and soaping his body all up. Dang it. What was wrong with her? One minute she was sorry he'd landed on her doorstep, the next, she was imagining joining him in the shower.

He strode down the steps and off her property. Her heartbeat settled down finally and she closed the door. She wasn't ungrateful for the work he offered, but it meant dealing closely with him again.

"Auntie?"

She swiveled around to find Ally in the hallway, her eyes half-lidded, her hair a curly mess of fluff. She stood there in her nightgown printed with tiny pink and white roses, her thumb in her mouth.

"Hi, Muffin."

She giggled softly. "I'm not a muffin."

"Oh, I forgot. You got up all by yourself this morning. Good girl."

Beaming, Ally puffed out her chest.

"Are you ready for breakfast?"

Ally's gaze darted around the living room. Every morning when she woke up, she seemed confused and unsure about all the changes in her life. At times, Susanna thought she was remembering her mother. At other times she seemed to be adjusting just fine. She didn't pressure her. She gave the child all the space she needed. "Okay."

"Great. We'll have oatmeal with fruit and then you can help me put muffins in the oven. Would you like that?"

The next thing she knew, Ally was racing toward her with arms outstretched. Susanna seared the sight into her memory. She squatted to scoop Ally up and spin her around. Giggles burst from the child's lips, revealing a mouthful of small, bright white teeth. Susanna was a sucker for that sweet smile.

It was the greatest feeling in the world. Having Ally's trust—and hopefully love—one day was all she could ask for. She wasn't Ally's biological mother, but she felt like a mom right now, and the feeling seemed to be growing every day. She brushed her lips to Ally's soft rosy cheek and then set her down. "Okay, my girl, it's time to start our day together."

"Hello, Austin," Casey said, climbing down from his SUV. Plucking off his Ray-Ban sunglasses and stuffing them into his shirt pocket, he extended his hand to his mentor. "It's good to see you."

Big, burly, sweet-faced Austin Brown clasped his leathery hand around Casey's. Austin's was a work hand, the rough calluses and blisters a permanent testament to the man's struggles and successes in life. He tugged Casey into a clumsy bear hug and gave him several forceful pats on the back. Then the former owner of Sentinel Construction pulled away and stared at him. "It's about time you came out to Sentinel Ranch again. Elizabeth's been asking for you."

"I can't wait to see her again."

"Well, let's head on inside. It's hotter than hell today. Elizabeth has a great lunch waiting for you."

Casey squinted to catch a quick glimpse of the sprawling two hundred-acre spread nestled in the heart of Crystal Canyon on the outskirts of Carson City. Austin had custom-built the mansion-sized ranch house twelve years ago; it was the envy of local landowners, Casey included. Constructed with flagstone, timber logs and brick, it was a visual masterpiece that earned a place on the pages of several architectural magazines. The publicity had done wonders for Sentinel Construction.

They approached the house and Austin turned to him. "You're looking fit. How's the back doing?"

"Most days I'm pretty good."

"Glad to hear it. Can't imagine anything worse than getting thrown ten feet in the air by a wild horse and landing smack on your back. Still makes me cringe thinking what you went through, boy."

"My life's different now, that's for sure. Mostly, thanks to you."

Austin Brown was a man to be feared, or so Casey had thought in those early years, when the older man had personally hired him in the rodeo off-season to work on a construction crew. Casey had been green around the ears and desperately in need of work to support Audrey. He'd learned a lot about construction during that time. Austin didn't like mess ups and Casey proved himself a valuable worker. After Casey hit it big as a rodeo rider and made a fortune in endorsements, he invested in Sentinel Construction and through the years, shared in the profits. Less than eighteen months ago, Austin retired and Casey jumped at the chance to buy him out with only one condition: that he remain as his consultant and advisor.

"You're the son he never had," Elizabeth had told him once. "He wouldn't want the company in anyone else's hands." Being parentless for most of his life, Casey was moved to tears by her comment and now he and Austin were as close as two people could be that weren't blood-related.

"How about you, Austin? That arthritis still giving you fits?"

"Ahh, I've got nothing to complain about." Austin's palm landed on his beer belly. "I've put on a few pounds since I retired though. Elizabeth's put me on some dang new-age regimen. Claims it's a way of life and not so much a diet."

Casey laughed. Austin on a diet? That he'd like to see. Austin loved food. Only his love for Elizabeth, his child-hood sweetheart and wife of fifty some odd years, could get him to abide by new eating rules.

Casey removed his hat as they entered the home. The cool interior walls of natural stone and wood were just as he remembered them. Casey felt warmth and love every time he entered the Browns' home. It wasn't picture per-fect. Elizabeth's half-knitted blanket lay on the sofa in the great room, her spools of yarn cozy in a basket beside it and a few issues of *Cowboys and Indians* magazine lay open on chairs and on their signature rock and glass coffee table. Miss Caroline, their black and white tuxedo cat, lay stretched out on the window sill as if she owned the place. Missy, as they called her, was going on eleven years and was the apple of Elizabeth and Austin's eyes. If it weren't for Missy, Casey would've brought the pup out to the ranch.

Casey lifted his nose to heavenly scents of tangy sauce and garlic and onions coming from the kitchen. "Some-thing smells mighty good."

"That'll be lunch."

The housekeeper stepped out of the kitchen and ap-proached him. "Hello, Mr. Thomas. Would you like me to take your hat?"

"Oh, sure." Casey handed it to her. She took Austin's hat as well. "How you doing, Bessie?"

She smiled. "Well, thank you. Miss Elizabeth wouldn't

let me touch a thing in the kitchen. She's making you one of your favorites."

"I told you," Austin said.

"Well, now that's incentive for me to come by more often."

"Wish you would. C'mon now."

Bessie moved on and Austin led him into the kitchen. Elizabeth was leaning over the oven, pulling out a roasting pan. She was dressed impeccably in a pair of beige slacks and a cream and brown printed blouse. Even working in the hot kitchen, not a hair on her silver-gray head was out of place.

The second she spotted him, she set her oven mitts down and lifted her arms to him. "Casey, it's good to see you."

He walked into her arms, giving the petite woman a gentle squeeze. His eyes closed to the tenderness swelling in his heart. Then he cleared his throat and backed away to look into her bright amber eyes. "Same here. You're as pretty as ever, Elizabeth."

"You're a charmer, Casey."

No, he wasn't. Mostly, he was gruff and rough around the edges. "I'll thank you for that."

"I hope you brought your appetite. I made you pulled pork with your favorite peanut coleslaw and fried onions."

Casey looked at the pan of steaming, fork-tender pork shoulder roast oozing with barbeque sauce, just waiting to be shredded. "I brought an appetite and a half. Can't wait to dive in."

Casey did the honors of forking the meat from the roast, working alongside Elizabeth, who was arranging plates for all of them. She gave Austin half the portion size she'd given Casey and left off the sourdough bun from her husband's plate.

She ignored Austin mumbling under his breath and smiled wide. "Okay, boys, looks like we're ready to sit down."

An hour later, after a delicious lunch spent shooting the breeze with the Browns, Casey sat in an extra-wide chocolate-leather chair facing Austin in his study, a tumbler of Scotch gripped in one hand. With its lived-in chairs, paneled fireplace and beige Italian sofa, the study was one of Casey's favorite rooms in the house. Walnut bookshelves banked two opposing walls. There were five hundred books if there was one on those shelves. Austin probably speed read through every danged book in here. Mesh window shades dimmed the sunlight but still allowed a stunning view of Crystal Canyon.

"So you're thinking of expanding the business?" Austin asked, eyeing Casey seriously. The older man had worked his fingers to the bone building the company from scratch and had a keen sense of business.

"Yeah, I've been shopping around Reno looking for office space. We're bursting at the seams in Tahoe and ready to branch out. But you know I wouldn't make that decision until I talked it out with you."

"Yes, well. I'm glad you did." Deep in thought, Austin scratched his chin, his fingers clasping the skin underneath. "You know that Nartoli nearly went belly up when he expanded too quickly. That's why I always tried to grow the business slowly."

"I'd take it slow, too. But I think the time is right." Casey put his lips to the tumbler and sipped Scotch.

"Do you have enough business in the area to warrant opening a division in Reno?"

"We're getting requests all the time and bidding on several big projects. Since the moratorium on commercial building has been lifted, the area is taking off."

"Smart of you to want to get in on the ground floor of that. Actually, you're young enough to do it. By the time those thoughts entered my skull, I was looking at retirement." Austin leaned into the arm of his chair and leather squeaked under him. "Tell me, Casey, do you have a girl? Any thoughts of settling down?"

Casey frowned. It was a question he didn't expect. A picture of Susie baking up those doggone delicious muffins popped into his head. "None at the moment."

None *ever*. But he kept that to himself to stay away from scrutiny or friends and family trying to change his mind. Casey had grown up really fast, raising Audrey and raising hell on the rodeo. When Audrey wasn't around, he'd led a wild life. There was always a woman around to keep him company. Funny, how a spill from a horse could change all that. He'd found out who his friends really were. Suddenly, the rodeo champion was a broken man facing months of rehab with no future to speak of and no hope of a family of his own. He'd faced that reality dead on and reinvented himself. It had been a large learning curve, but finally he was in a good place again.

"Only reason I'm asking is," Austin said, his eyes sharpening to Casey's doubt, "in those early years of building the company, I worked sixteen-hour days. Really put a strain on my relationship with Elizabeth." He rubbed the back of his neck and exhaled on a noisy sigh. "I've never told a soul this, but she almost left me. Gave me an ultimatum. It was her or my work. I chose her, of course, and began delegating duties to my staff. Turned out, by the time we'd agreed to start a family, it was no longer possible."

Austin finished his Scotch and Casey sat quietly, doing the same.

"I'll never forgive myself for that," he added.

Casey nodded. He understood better than Austin might realize about the impossibility of having a family. Still, something had to be said. He'd always admired the Browns' love and devotion and was grateful they'd included him in their inner circle. "You and Elizabeth have carved out a good life for yourselves."

"We have. And she loves working at the children's community center. She has those kids out to the ranch every chance she gets. It's a full life, but maybe different than she'd imagined for us. What I'm saying is, there's business and then there's family. Family trumps everything. Or it should."

Audrey, her husband, Luke, and baby, Ava Slade, were all the family he'd ever have. It was a fact. He wasn't fooling himself. "Gotcha. And I agree."

"Well, then. I'd say your instincts are right on. Go ahead and scout locations for expansion. And let me know what you come up with."

"Will do. Thanks, Austin."

"And we'll be sure to see you at the end of the month. Elizabeth and I will both be there. Don't you disappoint us now."

Oh, yeah. He'd almost forgotten about the Think Pink Strong banquet. He was being honored for his charity work. "I'll be there."

"That's fine, boy. We're looking forward to it." Austin winked.

An hour later, Casey said goodbye to Elizabeth, giving her a kiss on the cheek and shaking Austin's hand at the front entrance of their home. As he drove off, his head cleared of any indecision about his stay in Reno. He'd talk to his attorneys and make that expansion happen in the coming weeks.

Then there was Susie. That road was rockier. He'd kind of forced her hand last night, making her talk about things she didn't want to talk about. He'd done his best to explain his perspective and now that it was all out in the open, they had a strained, partially repaired friendship.

They'd even shaken on it.

But the memory of her soft fingers laced with his stirred up sensations that had nothing to do with friendship.

* * *

"She's adorable," Casey said to Susanna. They sat in folding chairs on her backyard patio watching Charger run circles around Ally. The pup was breathing hard and loving it. Susie's eyes stayed on Ally, who was giggling her head off.

Casey counted his lucky stars he'd let the dog out when he had. Ally had spotted Charger through the wrought iron gate that separated the Thomas and Hart backyards.

"Thanks. She's a sweet kid."

"It's rough what's happened to her. It's a good thing you're doing, Susanna."

She took her focus off Ally, who was busy stroking the dog's fluffy coat, to look at him. Progress. At least there was some eye contact now. But man, her gaze packed a wallop. The thumping should knock some sense into his brain, but instead, he kept staring at the soft grass-green specks in her eyes.

"I hope so."

"She seems happy."

"Right now, she is. That's because the dog is here. Some days I'm not so sure how she's doing. I like having her with me, but how stimulating is it for her being dragged from bed every morning to make deliveries with me?"

"You're doing what needs doing. Don't beat yourself up about it," he said softly.

"I know…you're right." Her eyes shifted to his. "Thanks. Sometimes I need that reminder."

A buzzer went off inside Susanna's house. "Oh, that'll be dinner. W-would you like to stay for some turkey meatloaf?"

His brows lifted. "Are you inviting me to dinner?"

She gave him a genuine smile. "Well…yes. I guess I am. But if you're busy, that's okay."

A backhanded invitation if he ever heard one. It didn't matter. There was no bleeping way he would refuse Susanna's dinner invitation, even after eating two of Elizabeth Brown's pulled pork sandwiches with all the trimmings at lunch today. He'd manage to fit a few bites in to earn a place at her table. "I'm not busy and I'd sure like to give it a try."

Her brows furrowed. "You've never had turkey meatloaf before?"

He shook his head and kept a smile on his face. Even if he wasn't stuffed to the brim, the idea of turkey as meatloaf just seemed wrong. "Can't say that I have."

"It sort of grows on you, especially if you smother it with ketchup. With all the sweets around here, I'm trying new recipes to make healthier meals for Ally."

"Sounds good." Whether it tasted good or bad, he'd be forcing the meal down his gullet.

She rose from her seat and called out, "Time for dinner, Ally."

Ally stopped petting Charger's underbelly and looked up from her spot on the grass. "Can Charger come, too?"

"I can put him in my yard and close the gate," Casey offered.

"No, it's just as well. Ally will never let it rest. She can play with him inside the house until I get the meal on the table." She called to Ally, "Yes, it's okay, sweetie."

"Yay!" Ally jumped up, a toothy smile breaking out on her face. "C'mon, Charger."

Susanna chuckled.

Charger trotted after Ally, and all of them followed Susanna into the house.

Just seconds later, Susanna shut off the egg timer, fit her hands into oven mitts and pulled the meatloaf out of the oven. A half-baked turkey concoction greeted her. She stared at the uncooked portion of meat. "Oh, no, not now."

Her shoulders sagged. Tears welled in her eyes as she removed her oven mitts and waved her right hand close to the opened door. She already knew the outcome. Her dog-gone oven was on the fritz. Where the elements should've been red hot and the turkey sizzling, the temp was luke-warm at best as if the oven had made a valiant effort before taking the night off. "Darn it."

This can't happen now. She lowered her lids and prayed to the oven gods for an easy fix. She had orders to fill to-morrow. And her new clients at Casey's job site were ex-pecting muffins in the morning.

Casey sidled up next to her and stared into the roasting pan. "What's wrong?"

"The meatloaf hasn't been cooking. My oven must've petered out halfway through."

"Do you know what's wrong?"

"It's happened before. Last time, I had to replace some fuses. But the repairman said she's on her last legs."

Casey blinked. "Mind if I take a look at it?"

"Not at all." She moved aside, giving him room to work. Casey had magic hands. Maybe they were good at coaxing an oven back from the dead.

He gave the oven a once over, tinkering with the knobs and inner workings, while she kept an eye on Ally playing with the dog by the kitchen table. A few minutes later, he walked over to her. "The bad news is, I don't think I can fix it. The good news is, I know someone who can."

He whipped out his cell and began punching in a num-ber.

"Who are you calling?"

"Our head electrician. He's been working at the restau-rant. If I can reach him, he'll come out right now." Casey turned his wrist to glance at his watch and she caught a glimpse of the time. It was past seven o'clock. She heard it ring and ring on the other end. "No answer," he said. "If he's still working at the site, he probably can't hear the phone. Let me try another number."

While Casey was on the phone, Susanna called the repairman from Speedy Service who'd come to her house the
last time. She didn't have any luck reaching him or the three
other repairmen she quickly looked up on her smartphone.

Shoot. This wasn't good. Her mind began racing. She'd
never failed to make a delivery. Not when her father was
ill, not after her mother had married, not when Ally had
come to live with her. Somehow, she'd always managed to
fulfill her orders.

"I can have someone out here first thing in the morning," Casey said.

"You don't have to do that. I'm sure I can reach someone
in the morning. It's just that…I won't make my deliveries.
And your crew won't be getting their muffins tomorrow."
She was kicking herself now for not investing in a simple
electric oven sooner. She'd been saving up to buy a digital
three-in-one convection oven with all the bells and whistles.

The puppy's bark broke into her thoughts. Ally's giggles
came next and Susanna broke into a smile. What a cute picture they made. Ally sitting on the floor cross-legged, the
pup on his hind legs, his paws on her shoulders, moistening her skin with doggie licks.

"Charger, down." Casey's voice was softer than usual
when reprimanding the dog. He shifted his eyes to hers.
"Little girl's best friend."

She chuckled. "That's one way of putting it."

His eyes lit up. He flashed a beautiful smile set off nicely
by his five o'clock shadow and Susanna took a steadying
breath. Oh, boy.

"I've got the solution to your problem. Wrap the meatloaf up and stick it in the fridge for tomorrow. I'm taking
you both out to dinner."

Four

Susanna sat in a semi-circular booth facing Casey with Ally propped in a booster seat between them. Cut crystal bottle lamps gave off a soft light that illuminated the booth and the bowl of fresh roses floating in water that sat in the center of the table. On the drive over, Casey had assured her that Michael's Steakhouse was a kid-friendly restaurant and Ally wouldn't be out of place.

Glancing around, Susanna noted a few other children at nearby tables and her shoulders fell in relief. There was McDonald's kid-friendly and then there was fancy, white tablecloth, kid-better-behave-himself, kid friendly. Michael's fit into the second category.

It still amazed her she was sitting here, having dinner out with Casey. She'd agreed without argument, not even flinching when he'd suggested it. She'd spent her time on the drive over here wondering why that was. Judging by the lift of his brows when she'd said yes, she'd surprised him too. Why hadn't she flat out refused Casey? She could have made peanut butter and jelly sandwiches and then called it a night.

The reason had hit her just as he pulled up to the valet parking area. Susanna was beat, mentally and physically. Her nights were long, her days even longer. She juggled her business and motherhood. Each day brought a new experience raising Ally. She was constantly second-guessing herself. What did she know about being a mother?

Tonight when the oven conked out and Casey took control, she was actually grateful, and her resolve had melted faster than a strawberry sundae on a hot afternoon. Her decision making skills took a short and much needed vacation. She'd caved because the fight was out of her and the thought of being served a delicious meal had almost as much appeal as gorgeous Casey Thomas.

Over her glass of lemonade she watched Casey dip his fork into his Caesar salad.

"Admit it, you were glad the meatloaf didn't make it to our plates tonight," she said.

Casey's lips twitched one twitch too many. "I won't admit that."

"But it's true." She couldn't blame him. Rodeo cowboys bred on beef didn't eat faux meatloaf.

"Not saying a word, Suse."

This time she didn't stiffen her back when he used her nickname. "I should invite you over tomorrow night, for day-old, reheated turkey meatloaf. That'll show you."

He laughed and then his eyes darkened. "Is that an invitation?"

Whoops. She hadn't meant to blurt that out. "Uh, sure." She shifted her gaze to Ally, who was content eating fancy breadcrumb-topped mac and cheese, a dish off the children's menu recommended by the waiter. "That's if I have a working oven by then."

"You will. I'll pull my electrician off the job if I have to."

"You want my turkey meatloaf that much?"

His expression softened and he blinked.

Darn it, she wasn't a charity case. A noisy sigh escaped her throat. "Really, you don't have to do that. I've got calls in to three repairmen."

"What about tomorrow morning?"

She moved pieces of chicken piccata around on her plate. "Nothing much I can do about that."

"Why not? I have an oven. The last time I checked it was functioning. You can bake at my house."

It wasn't a bad idea. But when she gave it more thought, her lips tightened and she shook her head. "I can't do that to Ally. I'd have to yank her out of bed at four in the morning and disturb her sleep." She glanced at her charge, still busy eating her meal, and lowered her voice. "She's just started sleeping better. I feel bad enough waking her up when I do and dragging her across town with me every morning."

"What if you didn't have to wake her up earlier?"

"Meaning, what?"

"You and Ally can sleep at my house tonight."

"W-what?"

Casey leaned forward, bracing his powerful arms on the table. A whiff of lime cologne floated to her nostrils and her senses heightened. He wasn't implying anything sexual, but her imagination took flight anyway. No, no, no, she screamed in her head.

"There are two extra bedrooms in my house. My folks' room and Audrey's room. You can have one or both tonight, and you won't have to wake Ally up before dawn. You can bake and make your deliveries like any other day."

She stared at him. He really didn't have five purple horns sprouting from his head, but you couldn't convince her of that right now. She began shaking her head. She leaned forward and whispered, "You can't be serious."

"Why not?"

Was he dense? She didn't want to sleep under his roof. With him only steps away. She wouldn't get a wink of sleep. But she wasn't going to admit that to him. She stared even harder.

When he caught on, he jerked back in his seat, opened

his mouth and then shut it. "Oh, okay. I get it. That's an easy fix. We'll trade houses for the night. I'll sleep in your house. Or get a hotel room for the night."

"I would never put you out of your own home, Casey. Really, it's a generous offer but…"

"There's no buts, Susie. You need an oven, I have an oven. You need a bed, I have a…" He stopped talking then and Susanna blushed. Casey grinned. "You know what I mean."

Why was he going to such trouble for her? Was it guilt or pity or something else? Casey had never been this accommodating before. Her lids lowered halfway. "Why are you doing this for me?"

He hesitated for half a beat. "Just being neighborly, Susanna. I've learned how to be a problem solver. Had to be for Audrey's sake. Your problem is easy to fix."

Now she felt like a jerk for questioning his motives. "Everything I need is over at my house."

"So we box it up tonight real quick and bring it to my place. It'll take us about ten minutes."

Us?

Susanna glanced at her watch. It was a quarter after eight. She could have Ally in bed by nine o'clock at the Thomas's place, and not have to lose a day's pay tomorrow morning.

She turned to Ally and smiled, softening her voice. She had to broach the subject lightly. "Ally, would you like to sleep at Casey's house just for tonight? You and I can share a big bed. Sorta like a fun sleepover. In the morning, you can help me bake using Casey's oven." Heaven help her, she didn't want Ally going backward. No big changes in her life, the psychologist recommended. This probably didn't count as a big change, but Susanna had to be cautious.

Unsure, Ally shifted her gaze to Casey.

He added, "Charger will probably want to sleep in your room too."

The child's eyes rounded to quarter size and she bounced up from her seat. "Can we, Auntie? Can we?"

Why hadn't she thought of saying that? Score one for Casey Thomas.

"Oh, well, yes," she said, meeting Casey's eyes. "Yes, I think we can."

Minutes later, Casey paid the check and slid out of the booth. He extended his hand to help Susanna and she took it casually, as if tingles weren't running up and down her arm, as if her heart wasn't thumping like crazy against her chest. She liked it better when she hated Casey and shoved him out of her mind completely. Now, he was back in town and her female hormones were acting like jumping beans.

As she rose and straightened, he released his grip and she found herself staring into his handsome face. She cleared her throat and took a big, hopefully unnoticeable, swallow.

Ally walked across the booth seat toward Casey. Instead of helping her down, he turned and pointed to his back. "Wanna ride on my shoulders?"

Ally giggled shyly and slipped Susanna a quick glance.

Susanna worried her lips. Was Casey up to this? It was obvious he didn't think he'd have a problem carrying the slip of a child on his shoulders.

She gave an encouraging nod. "Go ahead, sweetie. It'll be fun."

Casey turned and bent down, giving her his broad shoulders. "Climb on."

With Casey's assistance, she managed to wiggle atop his shoulders. It was clear Ally had never had a shoulder ride before. Her eyes lit brightly but with a hint of fear. Casey grabbed her legs to secure her and slowly rose to his full height. "All set? Here we go."

Ally giggled again. "Okay."

Susanna walked beside them, noting genial smiles from restaurant customers as they headed toward the front door. They probably looked like a happy family trio and for a few seconds, it was fun to pretend they were.

Geesh, what had come over her?

They reached the entrance and Casey bent his knees to clear the doorway. "Duck," he said to Ally.

It was great advice.

Susanna had better do the same.

Or she'd find herself getting knocked on her butt again.

By Casey Thomas.

It wasn't hard boxing up her kitchen utensils and ingredients for tomorrow's baking. Casey did the heavy lifting and the transfer went smoothly from her house to his. Getting Ally all cuddled in bed was amazingly easy since Casey Thomas, Ally's new friend and hero, made sure to put Charger's plaid doggie pillow on the floor of his parents' bedroom when he'd given her fresh linens. A blur of blond fur had bounded onto the bed as soon as Susanna had tucked Ally in. The two were becoming inseparable.

"Charger can stay with you for fifteen minutes," Susanna said.

A wide smile spread across Ally's face and she bobbed her head up and down. "But when I come back, it'll be time for sleep. Charger will have to sleep on his own bed. That's the deal, sweetie."

"Deal," Ally said, her little fingers rubbing the underside of the pup's chin. The dog was so content, if he'd been a cat he'd be purring right now.

Susanna left them and marched into the kitchen. Casey was leaning against the counter, one ankle crossed over the other, drinking beer, looking every bit as appealing as he had when he was younger and she was in love with him. He tipped the bottle toward her. "Want one?"

Her eyes fixed on the bottle. Yes, yes she did. But it wasn't a good idea—mixing Casey with alcohol. "No, I'd better not."

He took a long sip and her gaze flew to his throat as he swallowed. If only she wasn't so darned attracted to Casey, this being-neighbors-again thing wouldn't be so hard. Shifting her attention, she eyed the box sitting on the counter beside him.

"I should organize my stuff. Morning comes early for me. I hope I won't disturb your sleep."

His gaze darted down the length of her body in a quick scouring that melted her bones. A second whizzed by, then another. What was he thinking? "I'm a sound sleeper."

"T-thanks again…for dinner and for letting me use your oven."

He shrugged and set the beer down on the counter. "No problem."

When he didn't move out of her way, she sidled next to him and began taking items out of the box. Darn that cologne he wore. It drifted straight up her nostrils and would smother all rational thought if she let it. With jittery nerves, she pressed on. "I've got to get the butter and eggs in the fridge before they spoil."

"I'll help," he said, turning so he stood beside her.

He dipped his hand into the box and reached for the eggs at the same time she did. His hand brushed hers, and for a second she relished him touching her. His palm was calloused—probably from years of reining in broncs—and warm as a furnace. Hot tingles flew up her spine. "You don't have to."

His fingertip brushed over her hand as he pulled out the carton of eggs. "It'll go faster if I do." He smiled.

So many smiles from Casey lately. Her gaze dropped to his mouth. His lips were full and surrounded with pale blond stubble. *Sexy eye candy.* Mindy's words. Not hers.

She didn't want his help. He was a one-man wrecking crew and she was trying not to be wrecked again. But how ungrateful would she seem if she argued with him? She was barging into his home, taking up residence and usurping his kitchen. "Okay...thanks."

"Welcome," he whispered.

Susanna grabbed the butter cartons from the box and walked them over to Casey's refrigerator. Cool air blasted her when she opened the door. Glancing inside, she sighed. Poor thing was empty but for a few condiments, beer bottles and a partially used half gallon of milk. "Wow, and you're turning down my turkey meatloaf?"

He walked over and peered into his fridge. A deep chuckle rose from his throat. "I know, pretty pathetic. I haven't had time to do any shopping. And I didn't turn down anything. I'm taking you up on your invite for dinner tomorrow."

"You *shop*. As in, you buy groceries?"

"I wash my own back too."

She pictured him showering and silently cursed. What was wrong with her? "You know what I mean," she said softly.

"Okay, I admit to having my housekeeper fill my refrigerator and cook my meals when I'm home."

"So this is a new learning curve for you? I don't get why you didn't stay at a hotel near the River Walk. Would've been easier for you, I'd imagine."

Casey folded his arms and leaned them on top of the open refrigerator door. He was close, just inches away, and his gaze bore into her. The fridge temps were useless, doing nothing to cool her down. "Sometimes, it's nice to come home."

But, this hadn't been home for many years. "I guess so."

She walked to the tiled counter and began lifting the rest of the things out of the box. He shoved the fridge door closed and pressed his back against the counter again. She sensed his eyes on her, following her movements. Inside, her nerves jumbled. Why wasn't he leaving her alone? "Don't let me keep you from whatever it is you want to do tonight."

His voice deepened. "You're not."

Oh, boy. Heat rose up her throat. She gulped air and then turned to him, hands on hips. "Casey?"

He shrugged like an innocent school boy. "What?"

She blinked, but kept her mouth clamped shut. She turned around to sort her utensils and lay everything out.

"You're still mad at me, aren't you?" he asked quietly.

"No."

The sound of his footfalls approaching tightened her stomach. "Either that, or you just don't like me at all."

This conversation was headed nowhere good. "I...like you, Casey."

The warmth of his hands seeped into her shoulders. He applied enough pressure to gently turn her around. She faced him now but kept her eyes trained on his shirt collar.

"Prove it," he said softly.

If only she could resist him. But when his hands slipped to her waist, she leaned toward him. Another gentle tug and she was brushing her chest against his. Her lids snapped up and she found the sexy mouth she'd been admiring close to hers, his breaths warming her cheeks, the subtle scent of male cologne wafting in the air. He tilted his head and she eyed the firm slant of his jaw. Her heart spun out of control.

"I'm going to kiss you now, Susanna," he whispered over her lips.

He was like a gentle breeze blowing over her on a hot summer day...welcome and impossible to refuse.

He inched closer. She held her breath and closed her eyes. Then warmth touched her lips, his mouth a gentle crush of potency and desire. A tiny moan escaped her and blood rushed to her face. How utterly embarrassing it was, but wonderful too. Memories rushed into her head. She remembered his kiss. And the strength that seemed to pulse around him. His stubble scraped against her cheek and something powerful dredged its way to the surface. She had to kiss him back, to give as much as she was taking.

She pressed her lips to his and a deep guttural groan rose from his throat. The sound rang in her ears and her chest swelled. He tightened his hold on her waist and brought her closer. Automatically, she lifted her arms and circled his neck. He was strong and solid, bracing her as she leaned heavily against him. Stolen moments flew by as the kiss deepened. There were a dozen reasons why this was wrong, why she shouldn't be in his arms, kissing him, but there was one very good reason why she should.

She needed to know.

And now she did.

She'd hoped to be disappointed. Hoped that her fascination with Casey was over and done with. She'd hoped the taste and feel of him wasn't as exciting and intoxicating as she remembered.

But it was heaven, just like the first time.

Her body sagged. So much for hoping.

His hands were in her hair now, his tongue gently probing her mouth. She opened for him and he plunged inside, wrecking her even more with delicious sweeps. Her heart pounded fast, faster. She relished the feel of his arousal against her.

Without warning, he pulled his mouth away. Her gaze lifted to his. She already missed his warmth, the touch of his mouth on hers. Desire darkened his eyes and she drank it in, questioning him silently.

"I don't want to hurt you again, Susanna," he rasped over her lips.

How could she let this moment go? "Then don't," she whispered.

His brows furrowed and he shook his head. For a second, she thought it was over, until Casey's day-old beard brushed the side of her cheek again and his mouth came over hers, sweeping her into another kiss.

Every nerve inside her body pinged. His potent kisses opened her eyes to what was missing in her life. She kissed him back, her emotions stirring, resurfacing from a place long ago buried. She wondered what the heck was happening to her. She had no resistance against Casey. Her willpower was shot. Sure, she'd dreamt about him kissing her again, but the reality was much more exciting and totally frightening.

Casey pulled his mouth away and this time she saw finality in his eyes. "Damn it," he said softly. "What am I doing?"

His forehead thumped hers gently and he sighed.

"I don't know," she said quietly, her heart beating like crazy. What was he doing? Was she the convenient girl next door or was it something more?

"I do know one thing for sure. You're sweet, Susie." He gave her a heart-melting smile and then turned and walked toward the door, throwing a quiet "good night" over his shoulder.

Casey sat on his bed, his feet planted on the carpet and his eyes winking open as morning light invaded his bedroom. Mick Jagger's voice ground out "Satisfaction," an oldie now. Casey reached over and pushed the Off button on his radio alarm clock. It was early, around 6:00 a.m., and Charger, who usually nudged him off the bed, was nowhere in sight.

The pleasing scent of vanilla permeated the air and reminded him he had a woman baking in his kitchen this morning. Funny how he'd come to associate those sweet smells with Susanna. Last night flashed in his mind and he remembered kissing her. "Oh, man," he muttered. Why'd he gone and done that? He put his head down and rubbed the back of his neck. A little voice in his head told him because she was pretty and sexy and because he couldn't stand thinking that she didn't like him and didn't want him around. The more she'd tried to get rid of him, the more stubborn he'd become.

On a scale of one to ten, that kiss was an eleven. It was a damned near perfect kiss that got his juices flowing. "Damn it," he muttered. He should kick his own ass for being a darned fool. He should've just walked right out of the kitchen last night and not stirred up trouble.

He might have blown it, just when he was making headway with Susanna.

Twenty minutes later, after showering, shaving and dressing, he ambled down the hallway. As he reached the kitchen doorway, his eyes were riveted to Susie's cute backside—seriously fitted into tight blue jeans—as she worked at the counter. A Sweet Susie's lavender apron was hitched around her neck, with another bow tied just above her butt. *Don't be a fool, Casey.* He forced his gaze off her backside and toward the cooling muffins and cupcakes taking up space on his counter. Delectable, homey smells filled the room.

"Morning," he said.

"Good morning." She didn't take her eyes off the cupcakes. Using a cone-shaped thing, she made even swirls of icing around the cake top until they formed a white creamy peak and then moved on to the next one. It was a form of art and she was the artist. She managed to frost the rest of the cupcakes on the counter in a matter of seconds. Casey stood immobilized watching her work. "Vanilla?"

She shook her head. "Cream cheese frosting. Have a taste," she said. "Take anything you like."

He had last night and liked it way too much. "Okay, thanks."

He grabbed an unfrosted muffin instead of a cupcake and took a big bite. "Mmm," he said, "tasty. Let me guess, banana something."

"Banana-zucchini. Doesn't seem as though they would work together, but it's actually a great combination. The flavor of the banana and the texture of the zucchini make it a good seller."

Casey polished off the muffin in three more big bites. "I'll make coffee. Want a cup?"

She nodded. "Sounds good."

What was with her anyway? Cool as a cucumber, she didn't mention one word about last night. He expected weirdness. He expected recriminations. He expected some sort of reprimand. He had his defense all planned out; now it didn't appear that he needed to worry about it.

She began mixing up another batch of batter in a large bowl, carefully measuring out her ingredients. Her work would be cut in half if she had the proper equipment in a shop of her own. She wouldn't have to half-ass her business and could grow it to a much larger scale. She just needed the right tools. A dozen thoughts entered his head on how he could help her accomplish that. But now wasn't the right time to broach the subject.

He pulled the coffee out of the pantry and measured it out. Setting the coffeemaker to brew was a kitchen task he had mastered. One of the few. The machine grumbled and huffed and within seconds, steamy rich java trickled into the pot. The aroma, mingling with sweet pastry scents, rivaled the best cafés in the county.

The coffeemaker settled into a steady drip, drip, drip.

Casey grabbed two mugs from a cabinet and set them down near the machine. "How'd you sleep?"

"Good."

"And Ally?"

"She was thrilled to have the puppy in the room with us. She conked out, right after…after I came to bed."

She set the bowl on the mixing stand and turned it on low. The ingredients swirled around—chocolate this time, a thick fudgy concoction that clung to the blades.

He poured coffee into mugs and slid one over to her. It didn't look as if she had time to sit down with him, so he didn't ask. "Thanks. I brought cereal over for Ally. You're welcome to have some too, if you'd like."

"Maybe later. My electrician will be out here to look at your oven this morning."

"You got a hold of him already?"

"Yeah, I texted him five minutes ago."

She shut the mixer off, her eyes finally meeting his. "Thank you."

He didn't see condemnation in her gaze. She didn't utter scolding or harsh words. Maybe she'd enjoyed the kiss as much as he had, or maybe she wanted to forget it ever happened. Neither option overjoyed him.

"What time do you think he'll be by?" she asked, releasing the bowl from the mixing stand and deftly drizzling batter into the tins.

"In about half an hour. Does that work for you?"

She gave it some thought, her eyes roving over the counters, calculating. "I'll make it work. I need that oven fixed."

She lifted her coffee mug and formed a sweet little pout with her lips. She blew puffs of steam in his direction and he imagined it was her hot breath reaching out to him.

He grabbed his cup and took a hasty gulp. Hot liquid singed his tongue and he sputtered. "Ouch! Damn it."

Susanna's eyes rounded. "Did you burn your tongue?"

Her focus on his mouth didn't help the scorching pain. "You could say that," he snapped.

Her lips twitched. "I'm sorry, but I thought you knew how hot the coffee was."

"I wasn't paying attention." He was too busy noticing how hot she was. And it burned him. Literally. Susanna wasn't what he expected. She was more. And now he had the memory of kissing her to deal with too.

"Want a glass of water?"

What he wanted was out of Audrey's harebrained scheme. It was a noble idea to secretly help Susanna get on track with her business and get her bearings in raising Ally. Lord knew, he wanted to, but things were getting a little complicated and that could spell trouble. The last thing he wanted was to hurt Susanna again. "No. I'll live."

Susanna went back to work on her pastries. "Are you taking your run this morning?" She fit her hands into two oversize mitts and then bent to set the pans in the oven.

His gaze was drawn to her butt again. He had to stop letting it do that. He put his eyes back in his head. "No, not today."

"But don't you run every day? I hope my being here isn't disrupting your life."

She had no idea. "I made a promise to someone."

"Who?"

"Ally. Don't you remember? On the drive home last night, she asked if she could take Charger for a walk with me this morning."

"Oh, well, yeah, now I remember."

"You gave her permission."

"Sorry?" she squeaked.

"Don't be. I'm not in a running sort of mood today."

"Is it your…" If her eyes could reach around to his broken back, they probably would have. His back gave him some grief every day, but he'd learned to live with it.

"My tongue. Hurts like the dickens."

* * *

Susanna relaxed her shoulders as soon as Casey walked out of the kitchen. She deserved an Oscar for her performance this morning. Her pretending that all was right with the world had worked. Casey seemed to be expecting a battle or at the very least, a reprimand. When she didn't rant like a maniac about those soul-inspiring kisses last night, the question in his eyes had disappeared and he'd settled into his comfort zone. When he'd burned his tongue, she'd seen a moment of the old Casey, the gruff, rough around the edges, unpolished guy she'd remembered from her childhood. He'd been a bear raising Audrey, and Susanna had heard the brunt of her friend's complaints. This favor-doing, generous, puppy-rescuing guy was a mystery to her. Maybe his injury had changed him. The accident had been life-altering, taking the career he'd loved away from him.

It was also a mystery why he'd kissed her. She'd spent a good part of last night trying to figure it out and had come up empty. Maybe it was a spur of the moment thing; the mood had just struck him. But oh, that kiss had curled her toes and hummed through her body for hours afterward. It was high on her list of the best things in life, rivaling Godiva chocolate, Dom Pérignon champagne and a win on *Cupcake Wars*.

"Don't think about it," she cautioned herself.

Ten minutes later, after boxing her pastries, she walked into the bedroom to wake up Ally. She found her sitting on the dog's pillow taking up half the space, the pup taking up the other half. When they noticed her, two pairs of eyes brightened, one tail wagged and one little hand gave her a wave. A smile spread Ally's cheeks wide. What an adorable scene. "Good morning, Muffin."

"Auntie, Charger came on the bed and woked me up."

"He's a regular little alarm clock, isn't he?"

Ally's nose crinkled and she squinted. "A clock?"

"Because, he woke you up just in time," she explained. "We have to get you dressed. One of Casey's friends is coming over to fix our oven." She swooped down and lifted Ally up. "Your bath will have to wait until tonight."

After she dressed Ally and gave her breakfast, she took the last batch of muffins out of the oven, leaving them to cool on the counter, and then searched for Casey. She found him on the sidewalk in front of her house, talking to the man she presumed was the electrician. Holding Ally in her arms, she exited the house and approached them. Both men stopped talking and looked her way.

"Susanna, this is Theo," Casey said. "He's the best in the business, can fix just about anything. He's going to take a look at your oven."

"Nice to meet you, ma'am," the man drawled in an unmistakable southern accent. With weathered skin and graying at the temples, he appeared to be in his mid-fifties.

"Thank you for coming out on such short notice," she said, though the poor guy probably didn't have much choice with Casey being the big boss and all.

"No problem. I'll see what I can do."

"I'll take Ally and the dog for a walk now, while Theo looks at the oven," Casey said.

"Sounds perfect." It was anything but perfect. The damage was already done —Ally was head over heels in love with the puppy. Shifting her gaze to the child in her arms, Susanna said, "Sweetie, you get to take a walk with Charger and Casey. I expect you to listen to him and hold his hand. If Casey thinks it's all right, you can hold the leash for a little while. Okay?"

Ally couldn't nod fast enough. "'Kay."

Susanna turned to Casey. "Can I ask you not to go too far? If all goes well, I hope to be making my deliveries soon."

"Will do," he said. "Don't worry about Ally. We'll be

back in fifteen minutes." He stepped closer, his gaze directed at her child. "Wanna help me get Charger on his leash?"

Ally nearly burst out of her arms as she reached for Casey. He grinned. "I guess that's a yes," he said as Susanna transferred her to him. Ally clung tightly to his neck, her happy face peeking out from the top of his shoulders. Watching them walk toward the house made Susanna's stomach ache. She told herself Ally's fascination was only for the puppy. She wasn't falling for Casey.

And neither could she.

Susanna maneuvered her van through the city blocks of downtown Reno and found the construction site for Zane's on the River on First Street. She parked the van nearby and eyed the building. It was light wood and slate with wide window panels facing the Truckee River. The exterior design was amazing and appeared completed to her untrained eye. But she spotted a dozen or so workers entering and exiting the restaurant. Casey had said they were putting the finishing touches on the inside.

"We're here, Muffin. Our last stop of the day." She released a quick sigh. She was grateful for the extra work, but fatigue was catching up to her and she'd be glad when her day was done.

At least her oven was fixed. Theo didn't hold out much hope that the old girl would last much longer, but she was up and working for now. Susanna had been so grateful she'd given him a dozen double fudge brownie muffins to take home to his family along with a check for his services. The check he'd refused, saying it was already taken care of—something she'd have to discuss with Casey—but he surely appreciated the muffins.

Climbing out of the van, she opened the back passenger door to unfasten Ally's car seat and the sound of rushing current moving briskly down the river bombarded her ears. Susanna didn't come to the River Walk too often; her business was mostly concentrated in shopping areas and office buildings in another part of town. But hearing the mad rush of the river made her smile, reminding her of summer afternoons tubing the Truckee and swimming in the chilly waters as a kid.

Those were good days. Before the River Walk was built to its full grandeur with shops and restaurants and galleries, she and Audrey would come to the Truckee with her parents and have a ball. Her gaze flowed over Ally. She wanted the same kind of upbringing for her little charge. She wanted to provide her with summer days full of fun. She didn't want to cheat the child out of anything.

Grabbing two pastry boxes from the back of the van and stacking them in her arms, she and Ally headed toward the restaurant. Both wore lavender Sweet Susie's T-shirts. "Stay right by my side, Ally."

"'Kay," she said, and stayed close enough to bump legs with Susanna a few times. The kid really listened.

They carefully made their way past workmen and trucks as they approached the restaurant. Susanna spotted Casey in front of the double doors. "Oh." Her heartbeats ramped up. His back was to her and he was speaking to someone she couldn't see, but she'd know the cut of his jeans and the breadth of his shoulders anywhere. That mane of blond hair touching his shoulders was hard to miss too. Every time she caught a glimpse of him, she had the same darned reaction. He hadn't mentioned he'd be here, but then, she didn't really know how he spent his days. Overseeing the completion of the restaurant *was* one of the reasons he'd come to Reno.

She slowed her steps just as Casey moved to the side and turned her way. Her focus shifted to the man standing beside him. "Ah…oh, wow." A gasp swallowed her next words. *Oh boy, this was unreal.*

"Auntie, there's Casey!"

"Yes, that's Casey," she managed to whisper. With Zane Williams, *in the flesh*. Oh boy, she was a big fan of the country superstar.

Casey strolled up, casual as you please. "Hi. I see you made it."

She gulped, then nodded.

He lifted the boxes out of her arms instantly. "This here is Zane. Zane, I'd like you to meet my neighbor, Susanna."

He whipped off his trademark cowboy hat. "Howdy, Susanna."

Zane Williams had actually spoken to her. Thinking became a chore. "H-hi."

Casey set his hand gently on Ally's head, ruffling her hair. "And this little cutie is Ally. She helps Aunt Susie with the baking."

Zane bent to shake Ally's hand. "Nice to meet you. You like baking, do you?"

"Yes. I helped every day."

"Well, that's real good."

Zane looked up at Susanna and captivated her with his dark brown eyes. "I hear you bake some mean ol' muffins."

"Oh, uh, yes. I hope the crew likes them."

"The crew? Heck, I'm starving for one myself. Casey tells me there's none better."

She slipped a glance to Casey and he lifted a brow, studying her. So what if she was a little starstruck?

"Well, let's go have one then," Casey said. "I think Zane should get first dibs, don't you, Susie?"

She nodded. "Sure. Of course."

"Follow me," Zane said. "The main room is completely done. We'll eat in there, if you don't mind the noise."

This was totally surreal. Now, she'd finally have something exciting to tell her grandchildren. The day she got tongue-tied meeting her idol.

Susanna took Ally's hand and they entered the restaurant. She was immediately captivated by the workmanship and attention to detail in the interior. A cascading waterfall adorned one corner of the room made to resemble the Truckee River. Once the water was turned on, it would be magnificent. Teakwood and earth-toned walls brought warmth to the contemporary style. The buttery leather booths were enclosed enough to enjoy a private conversation without everyone overhearing.

Workman came and went. Voices and the sound of hammers banging away reached Susanna's ears.

"We've got a team working on the kitchen and a banquet room in the back," Casey said. "Then the appliances go in, outdoor patio covers go up and the place is done."

"Have a seat," Zane said, taking them to a corner booth.

Casey set the cake boxes down and helped Ally slide in. He waited for Susie and then took a seat next to her. Zane entered the booth on the other side. He began speaking again. "I never thought I'd be going into the restaurant business, but heck, I'm branching out. And I've got Casey here in charge. Anything goes wrong, I know whose butt to kick." A smile lifted his lips. One hundred percent genuine, he came across just like the charming man she'd seen on country music award shows. A few years ago, she'd even managed to go to one of his concerts when he was playing in Lake Tahoe.

"I'd like to see that," Casey said out of the corner of his mouth. "You've never whooped me, not once."

Susanna found her voice. "You two know each other...I mean outside of this project?"

"Hell, yeah, we do," Zane said. "We sorta came up through the ranks together."

"Before this guy got too big for his britches," Casey said, "he used to play at some of the rodeos. I had to endure his singing while we were on the road. That was what? Four-teen years ago now?"

"Something like that. I got lucky back then."

"Sure enough, you did. Now look at you, opening a dog-gone Southwest Asian fusion restaurant."

"The world didn't need another barbeque rib place." He laughed and Casey reacted with a shake of his head.

"Well, hell, I hope you know what you're doing. Hate to see this place go belly up."

Zane nodded, but the grin left his face and his gaze dropped to the tabletop. "I've been through much worse, my friend."

"Hey, man, I know."

Despite the background noise, stony silence deafened her senses. Just about everyone in America knew about Zane Williams's tragic loss. Two years ago, his wife and unborn child had died in a house fire while he was perform-ing in London. He'd taken it hard and had dropped out of the limelight, cancelling his European tour to return home and grieve. But last year he began performing again and his loyal fans embraced his return to country music. He was more popular now than he'd ever been.

Casey opened the cake box and shoved it toward Zane. "Have one. You'll feel better." It was a move only a good friend could get away with. Susanna's eyes widened and she held her breath.

Zane stared him down and then glanced at her. "Charm-ing, isn't he?"

She smiled. "You noticed?"

He smiled back and melted her country music-lovin' heart. Trading smiles with Zane Williams? She would've never guessed.

He dipped into the box and came up with her cinnamon coffee cake muffin. One bite and he began nodding. "This is really good."

"Thank you. It's a customer favorite. I'm glad you like it."

"Do you have a shop around here?"

"Not yet," she said, focusing on the sight of Zane Williams gobbling down her muffin. *Lord have mercy.* "I hope to one day. I run my business from home right now."

His gaze dipped to her shirt. "Sweet Susie's?"

"That's me."

"I like the logo. You'll get your shop one day. Just keep working at it." He shifted his gaze to Casey. "Have you invited Susie to the grand opening party yet?"

Casey's mouth twisted and he shook his head. "No."

Zane faced her again. "You have to come as my guest. I'd love to have your opinion on the restaurant when it's up and running."

"Really? I'd love to come."

"Glad to hear it. Casey, if we're all through with the briefing, I'd best be going. You three stay and enjoy yourselves." He rose from his seat, put on his signature hat and glanced at the cake box. "I think I'll grab another one of these if you don't mind." He decided on a double chocolate muffin. "Nice meetin' you, Ally. Susie, see you at the party."

"Bye-bye." Ally waved at him.

"Very nice meeting you too," Susanna said. Still in dreamland, she watched Zane walk away. "I should knock you to the moon for not telling me he would be here," she whispered to Casey.

"Didn't seem to matter. You charmed him silly," Casey said, his voice rough as gravel.

She blinked. "Did I? I wasn't trying to…I…"

"Yeah, well, that's the thing about you…you don't have to try."

Five

"So you're having my brother over for dinner," Audrey said matter-of-factly over the phone.

Susanna sat on the sofa in her gray sweats, feet tucked under her and cell phone to her ear, enjoying a few minutes of calm while Ally napped. She crinkled her nose. She loved Audrey to pieces, but she didn't want to talk to her about Casey. "Yes. On a dare. We'll see if he likes my turkey meatloaf. It's sort of a thing…never mind." She sighed. "I owe him more than a meatloaf dinner."

Her nose crinkled again. That didn't come out right. "I mean, he's been a big help these last few days."

"Oh? How so?"

Susanna explained about the oven repair and the offer he made to supply his crew with her muffins until the restaurant was finished. "And he introduced me to Zane Williams today. My gosh, Audrey. I didn't know Casey knew him at all."

"Well, he's building his restaurant. Of course he knows him."

"But, they're friends. As in drinking buddy friends."

"Yeah, Zane and Casey go way back.

"So, how's Ally doing?"

An image of the sleeping bundle popped into her mind.

"She's doing pretty well. Every day gets a little better for her. I'm happy about that. I think she'll like having a birthday party. Mindy is coming and a few other neighbors."

"It's a great idea and I'm sorry we can't come. Next weekend we've got a benefit dinner at the ranch. You know we'd be there otherwise."

"I understand. I didn't give anyone much notice. I got the idea just the other day. I want her to feel at home here."

"You're doing a fantastic job with her. I wouldn't trade motherhood for the world, but it isn't easy."

"Thank you, but you've got more experience at it than I have."

Audrey laughed. "Yeah, a whole five months more. I hardly think I'm doing fantastic. Yesterday, the little peanut woke me up in the middle of the night and I was so groggy that after I diapered her, I put her jammies on backwards and didn't realize it until the morning."

Susanna smiled as sentimental feelings washed over her. "I miss you living next door."

"I miss you too. Say hello to Casey for me tonight, will you?"

"I'll be sure to, Audrey. Say hi to Luke. Love ya."

"Love ya, too."

Susanna hung up the phone and bittersweet memories filled her mind. She rested her head back against the sofa cushion and thought about growing up on Meadow Drive, her parents, her friends. Her thoughts drifted to Casey and she remembered how much she'd always admired him. She'd hold her breath whenever he walked into the room and prayed no one would notice. Her crush was ruthless. She couldn't tell a soul about her feelings, but he was always inside her head. Lately, the night they'd shared hadn't strayed far from her thoughts either. It was hard not to get lost in the memory now. *She went to Casey's house in the dead of night, sobbing uncontrollably, sick inside after learning the truth about her father's illness. She needed comfort, needed to make the pain clawing through her gut go away.*

She couldn't face the agony alone.

Casey spoke gently and patiently in a tone that wasn't typical for him. She clung to him as they walked to the living room, her legs moving awkwardly and barely holding her up.

Casey sat first and guided her down. She plopped next to him, practically on top of him, the weary sofa cushions giving way from the weight. But she couldn't stand to break the connection.

He absently rubbed her bare arm. "I'll help you any way I can."

His strokes ignited a slow burning fire that seared away her pain for the moment. A slight lift of her head brought her gaze to his beautiful blue eyes. She raised her hand to touch his bristly cheek, then leaned in to touch her lips to his.

Too soon, Casey pulled back. "Suse, what are you doing?"

"Please don't refuse me this," she whispered over his mouth. "You offered to help me. This is what I need tonight."

When he started to protest, she answered him by sweeping her tongue over his bottom teeth. "Don't stop kissing me," she pleaded.

"Are you sure?"

Boldly, she slipped her hand underneath his T-shirt and caressed his washboard abs impatiently. "Yes."

"Damn." His fingers dug into her waist as he plunged his tongue deeper into her mouth.

His kiss left her wanting more.

His kiss told her he meant business.

His kiss removed any niggle of uncertainty in her mind.

He lay down on the sofa, pulling her along with him so

that she was pressed on top of him. He murmured in her ear, "This is crazy."

She lifted her blouse over her head. "Crazy and wonderful."

His gaze touched on her breasts in the white lace bra and her nipples hardened even tighter. And an odd thought struck—she wondered if she measured up to the women he'd had before her.

His eyes finally met hers. "You're pretty, Susie."

"I didn't think you'd ever noticed me."

"Hell...I've noticed. But you're my sister's—"

She put her finger to his lips. "Shhh...don't say it. Don't think about anything but this."

A hint of doubt crept into his eyes but then, as if he'd made his decision, he executed a perfect roll on the sofa that landed her underneath him. She took his weight, relishing the feel of hard muscle and gorgeous man. He rose up and his hands worked magic removing her clothes. She lay there nearly naked but for her panties. "Apparently, I'm not thinking at all," he murmured.

His mouth moved lower to brush kisses over her breasts. She didn't know such pleasure existed. Her back arched to offer him more and he moved lower, still planting hot wet kisses along her torso until he reached her most tender, aching spot and he kissed her there too. Torrents of pleasure ripped through her at lightning fast speed. Meeting her lips again, he kissed her as his fingers found her core and applied sweet pressure there. She shattered into a thousand pieces. It was heaven, this new and amazing feeling of complete release.

From then on, Casey treated her like something precious. Sheathing himself with a condom, he slipped inside her and she muffled a moan to hide the pain of stretching to accommodate him. She looked at Casey above her, his eyes darkened with desire, his face beautifully determined,

thrusting her, making love to her and tears filled her eyes.
Beyond experiencing the immense pleasure of her body
joined with his, she found the solace she needed to make
it through the night.

"Oh, Casey," she whispered, allowing the memory to
fade away. She'd always keep the secret of that night close
to her heart, but there was no going back. She had to deal
with the present now. She'd resumed a tentative friend-
ship with Casey and he was coming to her house for din-
ner tonight.

That was her new reality.

An hour later, when Ally woke from her nap, she helped
Susanna fill three online orders by carefully handing her
the muffins that went into each box. Susie was patient with
her and believed Ally enjoyed being her Aunt Susie's helper.
The time they spent working together created a special bond
between them. "Thanks for the help, sweetie."

Ally smiled wide, puffing out her chest. "I didn't drop
any this time."

Susie ruffled her hair. "No, you didn't drop a one."

Once all was set with the online orders, Susanna drove
her packages to the post office. On the way home, right
before pulling the van into the driveway, she caught sight
of Casey and beautiful, dark-haired Lana Robards sitting
on his doorstep, acting all chummy. The twins, Darlene
and Darryl, were happily distracted playing with Charger
on the front lawn.

Lana tossed her head back and she and Casey both
started laughing, her hand touching Casey's arm as if they'd
just shared a joke or something.

Susie clenched the steering wheel and gritted her teeth.
She pulled into the garage, parked the van and sat there,
battling opposing emotions. She should be relieved that
Casey had other neighbors to take up his time. She didn't

want him here. What difference did it make to her if Lana was talking to him? He could talk to or date anyone he wanted. She could deal with it.

Maybe he wanted to blow off their dinner tonight.

That would be fine with her.

"Auntie?" Ally's sweet voice broke into her thoughts. "Out?"

Geesh, a full minute had passed since she'd parked the car. "Yes, we're getting out. Hold on, I'll be there in a second."

She climbed out of the van and made short work of unfastening Ally from her car seat. Setting her down, Susanna closed the door and came face-to-face with Casey on her driveway. "Oh!" She jerked back. Seeing the puppy, Ally squealed and ran right over to him.

"Hi," he said to Susanna. "Did I scare you?"

She peered over his shoulder. No Lana in sight. "No, it's not you. I have a lot on my mind."

"Busy day?"

Well, yeah. Considering she'd woken up in his house, baked up a storm, made her deliveries, met a megastar country singer and battled shocking emotions seeing Casey talking to her divorcée neighbor. "You could say that."

He grinned and arched one brow, villain-style. "Are you trying to back out of feeding me turkey meatloaf?"

"No. I didn't say that."

"If you need a break from cooking, I'll pick up dinner for us."

Us?

"No way. You're not getting out of it that easily. Dinner will be ready in ten minutes, right on time. Was that Lana Robards I saw you talking to on your porch?"

What a dumb question. Of course it was Lana. Who else had four-year-old twins in this neighborhood?

"Yeah, she saw me sitting out front and came by to introduce herself. She sells real estate and gave me her card."

"How nice." Susanna slammed the door shut and averted her eyes. Lana would probably take up jogging next. Susie gave herself a mental slap. What was wrong with her? Lana and her husband had moved in at the end of the street a few years ago and shortly after got divorced. Lana kept the house, while her husband moved into another neighborhood close by. Through that time Susanna had developed a cordial friendship with Lana. Life as a single mother of twins wasn't easy for her and neither was juggling joint custody of her kids.

Casey tucked his hands into his trouser pockets. "Her kids are cute."

"Darlene and Darryl are a handful, but they are adorable. They're coming to Ally's birthday party on Saturday. I'm hoping they'll become friends."

"Birthday party?" Casey's tone changed. He rocked back on his heels. "You're having a party?"

Susanna snapped to attention. She hadn't meant to blurt that out. "Yes. I didn't mention it to you because, well… let's face it, why would you want to come to a three-year-old's birthday party." The man hung out with high-powered people, business execs and country superstars. Ally's princess party would hardly fit the bill.

His gaze shifted to the little girl petting Charger and giggling as if life hadn't dealt her a bad blow. "If the three-year-old is Ally, I'll make an exception." He smiled, a charmer that sucked oxygen out of her system. Why did he still have the power to do that to her? And why wasn't he busy on Saturday? Didn't women know what a catch he was?

Lana Robards did.

So do you, Susie. You dummy.

"Oh, well if you want to stop by, please feel free to—"

"I'll be there."

* * *

Casey brought in the last box of staples and baking utensils Susie had left at his house today and placed it on her kitchen table. "Here you go. Did Ally go to sleep?"

"As soon as I shut off the lights, she went right out."

"That's good."

"I still can't believe I forgot my baking supplies at your house."

"Not a problem," he said, watching her wipe her hands on a dishtowel. She'd just finished the dishes after giving Ally a bath and getting her down to bed. Susie's days were long, and something tugged inside him, seeing her working so hard, piecemealing a business that would have a better chance to succeed if she had a shop of her own.

Soft overhead kitchen light put a glow around her. She was as pretty as any woman he'd ever dated and had a lot to offer a man. Audrey told him she didn't date and that was baffling to him, but somehow a relief as well. He frowned as his thoughts drifted to last night and the way she'd kissed him.

He wanted to kiss her again. To wipe away the weariness in her eyes and ignite her body the way he had last night. Deliberately he'd kept his mind away from the night he'd made love to her, trying to forget his indiscretion and the pain he'd caused her. But watching her move around the kitchen now, her auburn hair falling over her shoulders in messy disarray and seeing her green eyes focus on laying out the tools of her trade for tomorrow's baking, that's all he could think about.

She'd been young and inexperienced, but by the way she'd responded to him, her body fluid and giving, he hadn't guessed she was a virgin when he'd taken her. Not until afterward when the evidence had been apparent and she'd admitted it to him.

Crap. But after all that he still remembered how good

it felt to be inside her. How soft her skin had been, how sweet her lips tasted. He watched her busy herself around the kitchen and remembered it all.

She lifted out a bottle of red wine from one of the boxes. "What's this?"

"For you. In case you want to take a break and have a glass with me tonight."

She read the label on the bottle. "Mmm. Sounds like heaven, but 4:00 a.m. comes really early in the morning."

"Is that my cue to leave?"

Her eyes lifted to his and she blinked a few times. "No. I wasn't hinting at that. You know what? Actually, I'd love to have a glass of wine…with you."

He moved closer to her and took the bottle from her hands. "You have a corkscrew?"

"I have one somewhere." She fished inside a few drawers and came up with one. "Here it is."

"You get the glasses and I'll do the pouring."

Two wineglasses appeared on the counter in front of him. After uncorking the bottle, he poured the wine and picked up both glasses. "Where?" he asked her.

"How about outside on the patio? It's a nice night."

"You lead the way." Casey followed her outside, his gaze wandering from the top of her shoulders, down along her back to her perfectly shaped butt. What was up with him? He couldn't get the vision of making love to her out of his head.

She sat on one end of a small three seat patio sofa, the cushions worn and faded. The sofa faced out toward the backyard. There was a crescent moon and the night was warm, but not uncomfortably so. He handed her a glass and then took a seat on the opposite end. Only a few feet separated them, but it was enough space to keep his hands to himself and his body from reacting to her.

"Thanks," she said, taking a sip of wine. "Mmm, this is good."

He sipped from his glass too. "Thought you might like it."

She leaned her head back and sighed. Her eyes closed. "I wanted to pay the electrician today, but he said it was taken care of. I want to reimburse you."

"No need. He's on the clock and works for Sentinel. He gets paid whether he's at the job site or somewhere else. It was no big deal. Besides, you paid him in Sweet Susie muffins, I hear."

"My oven is working again...so to me it's a big deal."

"Glad it worked out."

"Thanks to you, I didn't miss one of my deliveries today."

"You paid me back with dinner."

She turned to look at him. "I would question that, but you had two helpings of meatloaf."

"Yeah, I struggled to get it down." He smiled into his glass.

Her mouth formed a silent O and after a pause, her sweet laughter filled the stillness surrounding them. He chuckled and leaned back against the sofa, stretching out his legs. It had been a long time since he'd enjoyed being with a woman this much.

"The wine was a good idea." She took another sip and he watched her delicate throat move as she swallowed. "I don't get much time to relax these days."

"Can't imagine why not."

Her eyes lifted quickly with a flash of defiance. "I'm holding my own. It's not so bad."

"That's important to you, holding your own. You're more independent than I remembered."

"You only knew me as a kid. I've grown up since then."

He took a leisurely gaze over her body. "I've noticed."

Color rose up her cheeks and she paused. Then she dipped her head back and poured the rest of her wine down her throat. Turning to face him, she asked, "What have you noticed?"

Silently, he cursed. Those questioning green eyes were killing him. She was so pretty in the moonlight. Why in hell did he have to speak his thoughts out loud?

He began to shake his head. "You don't want to know, Suse."

"Maybe I really do." She put out her empty glass, waiting for him to refill it.

He lifted the bottle, glanced at her and then poured an inch and a half of wine into her glass.

She noticed his meager ration and lifted her brow. "Still thinking of me as a kid?"

If only he could think of her that way again, but brutal honesty poked him in the ribs. She was a woman now and he was struggling to keep his mind focused on anything but that. The more time he spent with her, the more he was tempted. Living steps away from her and seeing her everyday didn't help matters.

"Well, Casey?"

"Susanna, you've obviously grown up to become a beautiful woman. Independent, smart and nurturing."

Her expression softened and a bright glow entered her eyes. She scooted closer. Damn, his mouth was getting him into trouble. Casey had enough experience with women to know what that look meant. He went on, "But you work too hard. You deserve a life of your own. You've been giving and giving and taking nothing in return. Your stubborn pride won't allow anyone to really help you."

She blinked and then her mouth turned down. "I'm prideful and stubborn? Thanks for the brotherly advice I don't need."

Brotherly advice? That got his spurs jingling. "Well, what do you need?"

Seconds ticked by as she stared him down, her eyes packing a wallop. She sighed several times and he noticed her breasts rising and falling as they clung to her tight Sweet Susie's T-shirt. His groin pulsed and he went very still, willing himself to stay cool and collected.

Her eyes remained on his, daring him to back down. He wouldn't, of course. He was a competitor, or at least he used to be before he'd been broken. Old habits died hard.

"What I need for starters is another glass of wine." She shoved her glass under his nose and that ended the staring contest.

Casey pursed his lips. This wasn't going well. He picked up the bottle from the glass-top table and splashed red wine into her glass again. "Here you go," he said matter-of-factly. "You know, you asked me for my opinion."

"You told me I didn't want to hear it. That's a surefire way to hook me. I think you knew that."

"Maybe." He refilled his own glass and took a giant gulp, cursing his sister for her brilliant idea and cursing himself for going along with it. How do you help a woman who doesn't want your help?

She shook her head and sipped wine, as if it was the sustenance she needed to continue this conversation. "And *maybe* I wasn't expecting a lecture from you."

He leaned forward, holding his glass with both hands and swirling the wine in circular waves. "What were you expecting?"

"I don't know," she whispered. Then she sighed. "That's not entirely true." She turned in her seat, adjusting her butt against the corner of the sofa. "Why did you kiss me yesterday? Was it just curiosity?"

Casey squeezed his eyes shut briefly and gritted his teeth, then peered into his wineglass. "Partly."

"You can't stand it when women don't like you?" she asked.

"If you didn't like me when we kissed, then I'd want to be around when you *do* like me."

"At least you didn't tell me it was a mistake."

He kept quiet on that one.

"Never mind." She began to rise and Casey extended his arm, taking her wrist gently.

"I couldn't stand it that *you* didn't like me."

She stood above him and stared into his eyes. Revealing the truth wasn't easy. Touching her, too easy.

"Because I'm Audrey's friend and you wanted—"

"No, damn it. No. That's not it."

"Because you wanted my absolute forgiveness? I told you I'm over it."

He shook his head. "Not it, either."

What could he say? That he was on a mission to help her start up her business? To make her life easier for the short time he lived next door? That would go over like a lead balloon. But the lines began to blur in his head as to why he was touching her, wanting her genuine forgiveness. Hell, he wanted more from her in every way and it was dangerous ground he treaded.

"What then?" she asked, her sweet voice softening the tension in the air.

"Maybe your opinion of me matters."

His hand still on her wrist, he tugged her closer and rose from his seat. Their legs brushed and her gaze lifted to his. Crickets chirped and the sound of branches rustling in the wind caressed the quiet night. "Casey?"

A wayward strand of hair fell into her eyes. It was always doing that, giving the wholesome sweet girl a sexy edge—another reminder that she was all woman now. Lifting his hand, he brushed the hair onto her cheek. His fingers lingered on the softest skin he'd ever felt. It would be so easy to kiss her again. "Maybe I want you to like me for purely selfish reasons."

She tilted her head to the side, lowered her eyelids and focused on his mouth. The hungry look on her face nearly blinded him. "But that means…are you going to kiss me again, Casey?" The words, soft and whimsical, slid from her lips.

How could he resist her? He leaned in and touched his mouth to hers gently, giving her time to think it through, giving her a chance to back away. She answered with a little moan and her quiet cooing reverberated through his body like a jackhammer. He locked his arms around her and deepened the kiss, crushing his mouth to hers. Her passion shocked him and the way she curled herself into his body brought forth forbidden memories of making love to her. She was giving and warm and….not for him.

He remembered the reason he was here. It was hard to do, but he broke off the kiss. But he wanted more and couldn't seem to break away from her completely. He continued to hold her in his arms, tucking her head under his chin. He breathed in her vanilla scent. It made him smile. She was a sweet woman. Casey didn't do sweet. He didn't play with a woman's heart, the way he feared he was playing with hers, yet he forged on. The sooner he got her on her feet financially and any other way, the better. He could leave Reno with a clean conscience.

"Will you do something for me?" he whispered in her ear.

"Yes," she answered without hesitation. "What is it?"

Still unable to sever their connection completely, he pulled back enough to gaze into her eyes, his hands on her arms now. "Will you come with me tomorrow? I have something I want to show you."

Her pretty green eyes snapped wide open and a smile teased her lips. "Where?"

He took a swallow. "To look at some property."

Blinking, she stiffened and leaned back to fully gaze into his eyes. The smile left her face. "To look at property for your new office space?"

"No, not that. It's something else."

"What then?"

"I'll show you tomorrow. I'm asking you as a favor."

She moved away from him to set her wineglass down on the table. Out of the corner of his eye he caught her frowning. Her sigh rose up to his ears. "You're not going to tell me?"

"Will you trust me? It'll only take an hour of your time."

She glanced at his mouth, then up into his eyes. She was debating, and then finally she said, "Okay, I owe you more than a favor."

He didn't think fast on his toes anymore. He should have been better prepared. Or at least, he shouldn't have almost seduced her before asking for his dumbass fake favor. "You don't owe me anything, Suse."

Six

Gazing out the window of Casey's SUV, Susanna breathed in the new car scent of leather and chrome. She'd always loved the smell, but as pleasing as it was to her senses, her other senses told her she shouldn't have agreed to this. She'd almost made a fool out of herself with Casey again last night, practically asking him to kiss her. It must have been the lovely dinner and two glasses of wine that got her head all jumbled up. Why had he brought her wine anyway? Was he psychic? Did he know she loved cabernet, had been craving a glass for days and didn't like to drink alone?

"Does it feel weird not having Ally here?" He drove along the highway leading toward the River Walk area.

"A little. I've never left her before." She didn't have her three-year-old chaperone to keep her from making another "Casey mistake." It seemed that whenever she was alone with him, she did something stupid. "Mindy is happy to watch her, she says it's practice for her mothering skills. And Ally really likes her, so it should be fine."

Casey gave her a nod and turned into a parking spot on a residential street. She didn't know the street, but it was close to the River Walk area.

"Here we are," he said. He killed the engine and got out. She stepped down before Casey could open the door for her. She was curious about this favor but reluctant to spend any more time with Casey than necessary. She was crazy about him, or just plain crazy. And the more she was with him the worse it got.

"And just where are we?" she asked.

Casey moved beside her and put a hand to her back. His touch sent warmth spiraling up her back and she stiffened her shoulders to combat the glorious feeling. "You'll see."

Why was he being so cryptic? She had no idea what was going on. They walked up the residential street and turned the corner onto a busy boulevard. He took her hand then, entwining their fingers, and they walked past Beaut's dog grooming shop, On the Page antique book store and an adorable children's clothing boutique called Rainbows. "It's coming up." After another ten feet he stopped and turned toward the building. She did the same. Their reflection stared back at her through the empty shop window.

Oh, wow. They looked like a real couple, standing there, holding hands as if they were in love. She tightened her lips to keep Casey from noticing them trembling. Something softened in her heart. If only it were true. But that would never be the case. She couldn't put stock in Casey kissing her on two separate occasions. To him, it probably meant little. He was a man who'd moved in the fast lane. And she had Ally now to think about. The child needed stability in her life.

"Here it is."

She shook her head. "What am I looking at?"

"Sweet Susie's."

"I don't understand?"

"It's perfect. A good location for you to start up your shop. I came across it as I was looking for commercial property for my own offices. The Realtor said it's been empty a while, so you might be able to get a good deal on it."

"Oh...I..." Her dreams took flight and she imagined herself working here, alongside a few trusted employees. Efficient ovens and baking equipment to handle large orders would fill the back workroom. She envisioned the café-style tables lined up against the wall facing the bakery case. The walls would be lavender and white and she'd have daily specials posted on a black chalkboard for walk-in customers. For a moment and just a moment, she saw it all and it was everything she'd ever wanted.

By the glint in his eyes, Casey seemed to see it too. Why was her vision so clear to him? Didn't he know how painful it was to envision her dreams and not be able to act on them? "Casey, I appreciate the thought, but I can't do this."

"Why not?"

She began shaking her head. "I'm not ready for this."

"You're one of the hardest workers I've ever met. You can do this."

"No, I can't. I can't afford to open up a shop until all my ducks are in a row."

"What does that mean?"

"It means I practically have to prove that I don't need the money for startup costs, in order to get a small business loan. I've been denied on three separate occasions. Apparently, I'm not a good risk."

"I can speak with my banker and see if he'll cut you some slack."

"No, Casey. I can't let you do that. I appreciate it, though. I really do, but I'm saving up my pennies and it may take a while, but one day, I'll have my shop."

Casey stared at her for a moment, opened his mouth to say something and then clamped it shut. He nodded without another word. She lifted her lips in a small smile and slipped her hand from his as they walked back to the car in silence.

Casey rested his head on the back of the recliner, stretched out his legs and crossed his ankles. Pinching the bridge of his nose, he spoke into his cell phone. "Audrey, I'm not cut out for this."

"Not cut out for what? Shh, shh, now, Ava."

In the background his niece's tiny voice carried to his ears as she made sweet baby noises.

"What I'm trying to do for Susie. She's not buying it, little sis."

"Maybe you're not selling it good enough."

"I never claimed to be a salesman."

"Casey, you could charm your way into a convent if you wanted to."

Maybe the old Casey could have, when he'd been cock-sure and full of himself. But Casey had taken a hard hit that matured him and made him view life differently after his injury. He no longer played games with women to get what he wanted, even if the cause was just. If Audrey could've seen the momentary spark in Susie's eyes when she gazed into that shop window and envisioned it as her dream place, his sister would realize he'd done more harm than good today. Tempting Susie with what she wanted most, then see-ing the spark in her eyes die when she realized she couldn't afford her dream had been hell on both of them. The jab of regret that followed him home had made him pick up the phone and dial his sister's number.

"Shh, sweet baby," Audrey whispered to Ava. "I'm rock-ing her, but she's fighting me."

"Yeah, well. That's exactly what I'm doing with Su-sanna."

"You're rocking her?"

It was the other way around. Casey was drawn to Su-sanna and seeing her disappointment this afternoon almost sent him over the edge. He'd wanted to cradle her in his arms and tell her he'd give her anything she needed. That emotion scared the hell out of him and he'd kept his mouth shut for fear of saying something he'd later regret.

"Hell, Audrey, you know what I mean. She's fighting me. I'm imposing myself on her. I don't think she appreciates the intrusion."

"Nonsense. She's always liked you. I know she's glad you're there."

That was doubtful. Judging from conversations he'd had with Audrey, she didn't have a clue about the secret he and Susanna shared. Audrey would've brought it up to him, chewing him out in the process, and she surely wouldn't have sent him on this mission, if she'd known the truth. He sure as hell hadn't told a soul either. That's what made this whole thing so touchy. Now that he was here, he'd see it through for Susie and Ally's sake, but he wanted his sister to know how difficult it was. Wouldn't hurt if she suffered along with him. "She's not making it easy."

"I never said it would be easy. Susie is headstrong and prideful. The girl's been saving her pennies, but children cost money and so does running your own business. She's doing both and she's barely making ends meet. She gave up college for her folks, and now she's afraid to take a risk, because she's raising Ally."

"How do you know that?"

"We had a midnight conversation shortly after Ally came to live with her. It was a rare occasion where she let down her guard and told me some specifics. She confided in me, so don't you mention a word about this, but she's barely holding on financially. And she's running scared."

"She told you that?"

"She was drinking wine to my apple cider and it helped loosen her tongue."

An image of Susie's luscious tongue sweeping over his lips last night jumped into his head.

Crap.

He wasn't letting Audrey off the hook so easily. "You

should come down and help me out. Ally's birthday is coming up."

Ava's cries rang out. Right on cue. "I'd be there in a heartbeat if I could." Audrey's voice rose above the crying. "But Ava is teething something terrible. And the Slades are hosting a benefit dinner at the ranch this weekend. I can't get away. Why don't you bring Susie and Ally up here one weekend?"

The thought had entered his mind. He could drop them off and get Susie's sweet face and body out of his head for a few days. "She's working six days a week. It's hard for her."

Ava's crying ebbed to soft little sobs. "Hang on, Casey. I think she's hungry. Let me just get my blouse—"

He gestured with a wave of his hand. "TMI, Audrey."

She laughed into the phone. Sometimes he thought his sister enjoyed making him cringe. The baby stopped crying. "Okay, baby is happy now."

Now, a softer image came into his head, of his little sister nestling her baby in her arms and nourishing her. "Give her a kiss for me. And tell her Uncle Casey loves her."

"Ah, that's sweet. I will. Now, back to Susie...you've done a good thing, Casey. You got her some additional work. You've introduced the idea of her getting her own shop. That's a start. I hear Charger is making Ally happy as a clam."

"Good call, Sis."

"What do you mean?" she whispered. The baby must be falling asleep.

"Audrey," he grumbled.

"Oh, okay...I won't pretend I didn't know what I was doing. But an adorable puppy gets your foot in the door."

"I hope I can keep it inside the door and not jam it straight into my mouth."

She smothered a chuckle. "I have faith in you. How's work going?"

"Right on schedule. I found two locations that may work out for our Reno offices. Now, it's a matter of choosing one and setting the wheels in motion. The restaurant will be opening soon. I'll be going to the soft grand opening. After that, I hope to be heading home."

"Okay. Well, I have to say thanks for all you're trying to do for Susie. You know, you won't regret helping her. And brother, I know this isn't easy for you, but I trust you have a few aces up your sleeve."

"At least one more," he said. "And this time I don't see how Susie can refuse."

"Tell me."

"No. You'll find out soon enough."

"Casey!"

"Bye, Sis." He grinned and pushed the End button on his cell.

"Max, don't touch the cupcakes. sweet boy. It's not time for them yet." Maxwell Caruso's mother gently led him away from the dining room table before he destroyed the cupcakes that spelled out the letter *A* for Ally. Max was six and lived around the corner with his mom, Jackie, and his dad, Ryan.

"We'll have them in just a little while," Susie said. "Come say hello to Ally. Everyone is in the backyard."

"Sounds like fun," Jackie said. "Come on, honey."

"Some of the boys are tossing a football," Susie said, leading them out of the dining area. "Max, I bet you'd like to join them."

They followed her outside onto the patio. Helium balloons tied to the patio cover bumped in the breeze and a homemade banner that Susie had stayed up late to finish stretched across a wide beam helping to hide the splintered wood. Susie had meant to paint it, but that just hadn't happened.

Ally ran up to Max. "Hi," she said, smiling. "I'm a princess."

Susie was happy with what she'd done with the pink ruffle dress she'd found on clearance, a play tiara and two yards of tulle lace. Ally looked beautiful and the little princess stole her heart all over again.

Max squirmed around and stared at his tennis shoes. "Hi."

"It's Ally's birthday, Max. What do you say?" his mother prodded.

Still fascinated with his shoes, he said, "Happy birthday." Then his gaze lifted to the grassy area where Casey was throwing a soft spiral to Darryl Robards. Casey looked in his element, his mouth spreading in a megawatt smile as he instructed Darryl and another small boy on how to throw. He was obviously glad to find something to do that didn't involve face painting or pink lace.

Susie had resigned herself to the fact that Casey thought of her and Ally as friends. Why else would he come to the party?

"Is that Casey Thomas?" Jackie asked. "Oh, wow, the rodeo champion has come home." Jackie's eyes followed Casey's movements. "He looks…" she gazed down at Max and bit her lip, her eyes glazing over. "Healthy. The years haven't hurt him, have they?"

Susanna couldn't argue with that. There was no denying that blond-haired Casey, in crisp blue jeans, a black polo shirt defining his perfect form and well-muscled arms, had aged well, despite his injury. Still, every so often she'd catch him wince in pain, or rub his back. "He's here temporarily, staying at the house while on business."

Max ran over to the boys in the yard and little Darlene Robards grabbed Ally's hand. The two girls skipped over to the Pin the Glass Slipper on Cinderella poster taped to the wall.

"I heard he did really well for himself. He's some hot-shot CEO now?"

"Something like that."

"He's not engaged or married?"

"No…I mean from what Audrey tells me."

Jackie's lips curled up and her eyes drilled into hers. "So?"

Susie caught on and began shaking her head. "Oh, no…no. We're only neighbors," she whispered.

"Are you sure?"

She nodded quickly. "Very."

Jackie's smile thinned. "Well, darn. I'm usually a pretty good matchmaker."

"Trust me on this," Susie said, her nerves jangling. She didn't want any of the neighbors getting ideas or making assumptions. It was hard enough to deal with her own emotions regarding Casey, without having her friends intervene. "It's the last thing I need." She sighed and glanced at her watch. "I think it's time to play some games."

An hour later, Susie gathered everyone around the dining room table to sing "Happy Birthday to You" to Ally, and after she blew out her Cinderella candle marked with the numeral three, the kids lined up for cupcakes and punch. Ally was the first in line.

Susanna was aware of Casey hanging in the back of the room, leaning against the wall, ankles crossed. She made the mistake of looking into his eyes. He arched a brow and his mouth cocked up. The hand she had on Ally's special cupcake trembled, the cupcake tipped and she fumbled with it. She caught it just in time. Images of the cupcake sitting upside down in a pool of chocolate frosting flashed in her head. Darn him. He'd told her he had something special for Ally and he'd bring it by after the party. Now, her curiosity was killing her. "Here you go, Princess Ally. You get the first one."

"The one I baked all by myself?"

"Yes, sweetheart. It's the one you made. Look, see the pretty princess ring right on top?"

Ally's eyes sparkled as Susanna handed over the cupcake. The joy on her daughter's face filled her heart.

Daughter.

It was the first time Susanna had actually thought of her that way. Sweet sensations whirled in her belly. They were becoming a family. She'd never expected this deep love to consume her, but now that she had Ally, she wouldn't trade her life with anyone. It was her and Ally against the world.

Susanna doled out the cupcakes one at a time to the children first, and then served the adults. She was glad to see a handful of clients she'd invited had come to the party, along with neighbors her family had been close to through the years. She wanted everyone to get to know Ally. It was important that she fit in and have friends.

After everyone was served cupcakes, her guests dispersed and Susanna was about to join them outside when Darryl Robards popped his head up by the table again. "Can I have another? One with silver swords this time?"

The prince swords and princess rings made of fondant were totally edible, but packed with enough sugar to fuel an army of little boys and girls. "I suppose you can have another if your mother says it's okay."

Susie lifted her head, searching for some sign of Lana, and found her instantly. She was sitting on the living room sofa next to Casey, the two looking very cozy. Lana flipped her long mane of dark hair over her shoulder as she focused on what Casey was saying. As if he was the most important man in the world. Susie's stomach pinged. She fisted her hand to keep it from reflectively going there. Sharp irrational emotions tunneled through her system, watching the two of them thoroughly engaged in conversation. Lana was a natural with men. She had all the right words and knew how to capture a man's attention.

"Here, hon," Mindy said, nudging Susanna. "You forgot to serve the punch. Let me help you." She picked up a ladle and filled a few cups.

"Oh, uh. Thanks."

"Darryl, why don't you go ask your mother if you can have another cupcake," Mindy said.

"Okay!"

Mindy leaned in to whisper, "That should break up their little huddle."

"It's none of my business," Susie mumbled.

"Sure thing, sweetie. And I've just swallowed a soccer ball."

A quick glance at her friend's belly had her smiling. "Does the soccer ball have a name?"

"Don't change the subject," she hissed. "You're green."

Susie shook her head and but it was no use trying to deny what she was feeling. She hated thinking of Lana hooking up with Casey. That pill would be hard to swallow. "I can't do anything about it."

"Says who?" Mindy ladled punch into two more cups and set them onto a plastic fairytale princess tray.

"Says me." Susanna had no options when it came to Casey. Though she'd secretly loved and despised him, depending on the day you asked her, she knew that road only led to destruction. "I have Ally now. She's my main focus."

"As it should be, but you deserve a little fun, too, you know. You give and give."

Susie sighed. "It's a fatal flaw."

"So why not take a little? No one deserves it more than you."

"I'll think about it, Mindy." The trouble was, she had been thinking about Casey. Too much. Some days she didn't mind getting out of bed at an ungodly hour in anticipation of seeing Casey Thomas jog by her house. She'd peek out her kitchen window hoping to catch a glimpse of all six feet two inches of him, working up a sweat.

Susie lifted the tray of filled punch cups and headed outside. Walking onto the patio, she announced, "Punch time, kids." She hoped Lana got the hint. The party was outside...with the children.

Ally barreled into Casey's legs at the foot of his garage and her unexpected outburst of affection had him bending on one knee to accept her tight hugs. "Does this mean you like your present?"

Ally's head immediately bobbed up and down. The tulle train attached to her tiara loosened and fell to the ground. Ally didn't notice. Giggling and pointing, she focused on the gift she'd just been given. "Lookee, Auntie. Lookee!"

"I see it, Muffin." Susie stared at a glossy stainless steel double-wide oven wrapped in a giant bubblegum-pink bow. Her heart began racing. The digital, three-way oven had every feature known to man, or at least to the baking world. Lost in the moment, Susie pictured herself standing over the oven with Ally by her side as they worked together. But then reality seeped in. She couldn't allow this. She sent Casey a firm look. "It's...it's very generous of Casey."

He kept his focus on Ally. Was he deliberately refusing her eye contact?

Heck yeah, he was.

She blinked, trying to find words that wouldn't hurt Ally. What was Casey thinking, giving an oven as a birthday gift? He had no right doing this. He should've consulted her. She wouldn't have allowed him to buy such an expensive gift. Good deed or not, she wasn't a charity case. But how could she send it back now that Ally had seen it?

Casey had her boxed in a corner.

"If your auntie says it's all right," Casey said to Ally, "I'll have the new oven moved into your house tonight. You can help your auntie bake tomorrow."

"I frosted cupcakes for my party."

"I know you did. They were delicious. You're the best baker's helper. And now you have an oven that will work every time." Casey smiled at Ally, giving her one last squeeze before rising up. Finally, he met Susanna's eyes. "So, is it okay?"

"Is it, auntie?" Ally bounced up and down, smiling and bobbing her head. "Is it?"

What could she say? How could she disappoint her little girl on her birthday? Debating with herself, she peered at Casey a long moment. He stared back, locking eyes with her. She found no smugness in the tilt of his chin or satisfaction written on his face. Instead, she saw hope glisten in those deep azure eyes.

The same hope registering on Ally's expectant face.

Susanna's shoulders fell, not in defeat or resignation. Oddly, she felt a sense of liberation in allowing herself to accept this gift. A sigh whispered from her lips. "Yes. It's okay, Casey. Thank you."

He nodded.

"But I would like to talk to you about this later."

"I figured." He grinned. "Hey, Ally, I have one more present for you."

Rosy color brightened her cheeks. "You do?"

"It better not be a puppy," Susie muttered.

Ally didn't seem to hear, but Casey's mouth quirked up. "Don't worry." With a remote control, Casey beeped the trunk of his SUV open, revealing a big box professionally wrapped in cotton candy pinks and powder blues. Casey hoisted the box from the back.

"Might be better to open this in the house," he said. "It's heavy for you two."

Well, thank goodness, it wasn't a dog. At this point, she didn't know what Casey had up his sleeve. Or in his arms.

"Follow me," Susanna said.

Minutes later, Casey and Susanna looked on from the sofa as Ally knelt on the living room floor and ripped away at the prettily wrapped package. Ally's eyes widened when she unwrapped the gift and saw the colorful images on the bulky box. "Oh! Auntie, Auntie…lookee. A princess dream castle!"

"I see it. Ally, it's beautiful. Looks like there's a fairy princess doll in there too."

Susanna slid to the floor and helped Ally open the flaps on the box. It contained a nine-room dollhouse, completely furnished, including a winding staircase and a set of clothes for the crimson-haired doll.

"Be sure to thank Casey for your present, Ally."

"Thank you," she squealed, too enraptured with the gift to give Casey a glance.

"You're welcome, Ally. I'm glad you like it. Happy birthday." Casey rose from his seat. "Well, I'd better get going. I'll call my installer and have—"

Susanna rose too. "Wait just a sec, Casey. I have some extra muffins to give you in the kitchen. Ally, will you play here for a few minutes with your new things while I talk to Casey?"

"'Kay!"

Susie marched into the kitchen, keeping her eyes peeled on the old clunker oven that had served her well over the years. Only lately had the ol' girl begun to fail her. She tamped down her mounting frustration at her own helplessness over this situation—she'd been saving up for a new oven, but it was admittedly going slowly because there was always something else that needed doing. Something costly. She squeezed her eyes closed and reminded herself Casey had done a good thing.

When she whirled around, Casey was leaning against the counter, arms folded around his middle.

"I'm ready to take my *muffins*."

"I bet you are."

He gave her a quick grin.

"This is hard for me, Casey. I know you mean well, but do you have any idea how I feel not being able to provide for Ally the way I want to?"

He shook his head and pushed away from the counter. He sauntered over to her and stopped inches from her face. She gazed at him, touched by the shocking sincerity rimming his eyes. "You're providing for Ally just fine, sweetheart."

"No, I'm not. I can barely…"

"Ally is happy. That's a remarkable feat, after what she's been through. And you're making that happen."

"Am I?" Her eyelids fluttered. She needed to hear those assurances now. "That's the most important thing."

"It is." There was a gentle look in his eyes now.

"The oven is a generous gift, but I can't deny my pride's suffering a little bit."

Casey entwined their fingers, his thumb playing softly over her skin and giving her goose bumps. "Your pride shouldn't be suffering, Suse. Mine should. Your folks took Audrey in, housed her, looked after her and fed her on too many occasions to count. Hell, I'm remembering how many times they sent me food too, when I was in town. The Thomas family is responsible for a lot of the wear and tear on that ol' oven."

"My folks did it out of the goodness of their hearts, Casey."

"Now let me do the same."

She'd never stopped to think about it from Casey's point of view. Now that she did, she understood his measure of pride too. Susanna chewed her lip, drawing his attention. A hungry gleam entered his eyes. He brought her hand to his lips and brushed it with a soft kiss.

"Oh, Casey. I don't know how to thank you."

Grasping her hand tighter, he gave a tug. She fell into his chest, the tips of her breasts flattening against hard muscle. A slow burning fire twitched between her legs.

"I can think of a way." His breath fanned her cheeks and when he turned his head, his beautiful mouth captured her lips. The taste of him combined with his heady male scent turned her inside out. She was stuck on a fickle elevator of emotions, shooting up, then plunging down, then up again.

Her hands flew to his hair, the long locks a thrill to comb through with needy fingers. He walked her backward and the cool texture of the kitchen wall halted his pursuit. He trapped her there with the firm stance of his body, bracing his hands on the walls. She welcomed the pulsing heat surrounding her.

The kiss deepened as he swept his tongue over her lips and into her mouth. The ache between her legs began to throb. This was crazy. Insane. Her breaths heaved hard, nearly bursting from her chest.

Suddenly, Casey dropped his hands and rolled away, so that his back was to the wall as well. As they stood side by side, a clunk resounded in the room—it was his head hitting the wall. He reached for her hand again, his grasp loose this time, but seemingly necessary. Staring straight ahead, he said, "I wasn't bartering an oven for sex. I hope you know that."

She didn't doubt it. If anything, Casey was overly cautious around her, which made this whole thing even more astonishing. He certainly didn't need to barter anything for sex. Not with the way the single women at the party were flirting with him today. "I do know that."

"I got caught up in…"

"The moment?"

"In you," he rasped.

Susie squeezed her eyes shut. Her pulse went on a wild jumping spree. Casey knew how to thrill. He knew just the right words to make squash of her brains, too. He was gifted with that particular trait, but was she fooling herself into believing him?

She was well aware of Ally playing in the next room. She was also well aware that whatever was happening between her and Casey, she didn't want it to end. What had Mindy said today? She deserved a little fun in her life. But dare she chance it? She turned her head and gazed at his pronounced profile. "Casey?"

His head met with the wall again. Thump. Then he turned her way. "I'm thinking I could stop by tonight with a bottle of wine after Ally goes to bed."

She took a deep breath and blew it out softly. "I wouldn't turn you away."

He winced, as if he had been expecting a refusal. The pain reached his eyes as he stared at her for a long moment. She found more questions there than answers. Then he nodded and pushed himself away from the wall. She watched him saunter out of her kitchen and exit the house, her heart pounding up in her ears.

Seven

"Okay, that's the end of storytelling," Susanna whispered, closing the Dr. Seuss book. Ally had fought against sleep, but she'd finally lost the battle. Her eyelids lowered gently and Susanna tucked her into her covers and kissed her on the forehead. "Good night, big girl. You had a busy day."

"Uh…huh." Her tiny breaths instantly became steady and her head fell to the side of her pillow.

Susanna smiled and rose quietly. Setting the switch of Ally's Tinkerbell lamp to nightglow, an amber hue settled on the room and she tiptoed out, shutting the door partway.

As soon as her feet hit the hallway floorboards, her nerves rattled.

Would Casey actually come over tonight?

Susie walked into her bedroom, plopped down on the bed and picked up her cell phone to put in a quick call to her mom, something she liked to do several times a week. Her mother had called earlier to wish Ally a happy birthday and Susie promised to call her back tonight after the party. Things always seemed better after she spoke with her mother. Tonight especially, if even just for a minute or two, she needed to hear the soothing tone of her mother's voice.

When Susanna got through, her mother said, "I'm sorry I had to miss Ally's birthday party."

"It's okay, Mom. She loved the doll you sent her."

"That makes me happy. So, all went well?"

"Mom, I think Ally had a great time."

"Oh, that's wonderful, honey."

After a few minutes rehashing the games, the cupcakes, the guests in attendance, Susie said good-night to her mother and ended the call.

With a turn of her head, she caught her reflection in the mirror and cringed. The ghastly person staring back at her had a chalky complexion, smudged eyeliner and hair in a tangle. "Oh, no...."

Lifting the hem of her blouse, she counted four stains; at least two of them were identifiable as chocolate. Had she gone around looking like this all day?

Geesh.

She bounded up from the bed, stripped off her clothes and jumped into the shower. A warm refreshing spray hit her body and sank into her bones. She soaped up and scrubbed her hair and then after the shower, poured vanilla-scented lotion all over her skin. She picked out her clothes, but nothing too adventurous—a pair of snug-fitting black jeans and a clean Sweet Susie's T-shirt that she decided to tuck into her waistband.

Ambling to the kitchen she did a double take, seeing the stainless steel appliance where her mother's oven once sat. It was shocking, but in a good way. It definitely added contemporary style to the workspace. She couldn't wait to try it out. Just as Casey promised, the installer had come an hour after the party ended and hooked it up.

Now glancing at the digital clocks on the microwave above and oven below, she had two reminders of the time. It was well after nine. Fear mingled with relief. What if he didn't come? What if he did?

A sudden droning buzz from the tile counter made her jump. She glanced at the source of the sound...her cell phone. Relaxing her shoulders, she picked it up and viewed the screen. It was a text from Casey. Is it too late to come over?

Her great relief surprised her. She didn't know how she'd face him if he'd stood her up. A new sort of trembling took hold and she breathed in steadily to calm her jittery nerves.

She stared at the message. Thankfully, tomorrow was Sunday and not a work day. She'd hoped to spend part of the day experimenting with the oven, but other than that, she had no excuse to give him except that it was a ludicrous idea. She punched in her reply. Do you have wine?

Seven-year-old cab, he texted back.

Come over. Susie's fingers trembled as she typed in the words, then hit Send.

Now, it was too late to back out. She hadn't done an impetuous thing in all of her adult life. The last time she had, she'd been eighteen and it had been with Casey. Was history repeating itself?

Two minutes later she heard a soft knocking on the back door. Casey had discreetly come through their backyards. She walked over to open the door and true to his word, he stood on the shadowy porch holding a bottle of claret wine and two goblets that twinkled in the moonlight.

"Hi," she whispered. "Come inside."

Silently, he entered the house and waited for her to close the sliding glass door. When she turned, Casey stood in the shadows towering over her.

"Would you like to sit down?" she asked.

Opting to keep the lights off, she drew the drape all the way open, and an infusion of pale moonlight skimmed the room.

She took her seat first. The sofa creaked beside her when he sat in the same spot where he'd been speaking with Lana today. He placed the wine and glasses on the cocktail table and then turned to her. "Is Ally sleeping?"

"Yes, she's out. She had a big day."

He nodded. "So did you. Are you exhausted?"

Yes, she was pooped, but not too tired to spend private moments with him. She sighed and told the truth. "A little. The wine will help."

"I uncorked it at my house. It's had time to breathe." Leaning forward, he poured wine into each glass and handed one to her.

"Thanks."

"Wanna toast Ally's birthday?"

"Of course," she whispered. "As long as I can toast your generosity too. The oven was installed after dinner. I still can't believe it. You must've pulled some strings to get an installer out here on a Saturday night."

"Maybe one or two. It was worth it," he said quietly.

"Ally was thrilled at the gifts you gave her." So was she. The new oven meant stability and peace of mind for her. She couldn't wait to get her hands on it to bake something fantastic. She offered up a toast. "To Ally and to you."

Casey met her glass with the softest clink and then brought the goblet to his mouth.

She sipped her wine. "This is delicious," she said, studying the ruby liquid in her glass. She was no great connoisseur, but the wine was as pungent as the earth with a hint of oak and berries.

"It's from my friend's wine cellar." Crossing one leg over his knee, he leaned back against the sofa cushion and relaxed.

"That's a great friend," she said, savoring the flavor.

"He is. He and his wife are good people. He owned Sentinel before I took over. He's taught me just about everything I know about the business. Austin and I go way back to when I was a young pup learning the ropes."

"You met him at the rodeo?"

"No, not exactly. I met him accidentally. It was after the

rodeo in Carson City. Man, I was in a hellfire hurry to get home that night, when I saw this Cadillac broken down on the highway. I could tell the driver didn't know squat about cars from the way he was trying to open the hood. It wasn't in me to drive by and leave him and his wife stranded on the deserted highway. I stopped to help him out. Turned out his car needed a jump and I helped get the car started for them. I was ready to climb back into my rattletrap of a truck, when the man offered to buy me dinner. Of course, I refused. Audrey needed me and I explained to him about the younger sister I was trying to raise on my own. She was sick at home with a virus and waiting on me. That impressed the hell out of him, he admitted to me later. I'll never forget the look of regard in his eyes right before he handed me his business card. He told me I had a job if I ever needed one in the off season. All I had to do was give him a call. Which I did." Casey's gravelly voice took on a reverent tone. "Meeting him changed my life."

Susanna sipped wine, listening as he continued to talk about his past, about how he'd feared he was messing up Audrey's life, about how he didn't know if he'd done right by her completely. Sometimes his rigid rules had only made Audrey rebel more.

Susanna had always taken Audrey's side, even as infatuated as she'd been with him, but now she understood his motives and couldn't find fault with him. Well…not so much.

As crazy as it seemed, Casey put her at ease tonight. The hunk of a man sitting beside her, who'd kissed her senseless earlier in the day, was also capable of soothing her frazzled nerves. He was giving her a better understanding of who Casey, the man, actually was. She was so wrapped up in his stories, an entire hour flew by.

When Casey stopped speaking and they'd finished the wine, he reached over and linked their fingers together.

Warmth seeped into Susanna's bones. Her heart pounded. She feared taking a swallow because the noise might break the moment. She felt connected to Casey right now and welcomed the sensations rippling through her.

He leaned over and kissed her, gently, sweetly, brushing his lips over hers. "I don't think I've ever told anyone those things," he whispered.

"I'm glad you told me."

"Are you?" He stared at her lips, his voice a deep rasp. "And you've forgiven me?"

"Yes. I've told you that before."

"I don't want to make another mistake with you."

"It was a long time ago. We've both changed."

"Yeah." Casey touched her face, his index finger tracing along the line of her cheek. His eyes darkened and his head tilted again as he brought his mouth down on hers. She heard a breathy gasp and for a second she didn't know if it came from him or her, until the reverberation echoed again inside her throat.

"I like the sounds you make." His grin could destroy her heart.

She shook her head. "I'm definitely not smooth." Not like Lana Robards.

"Maybe that's what I like best about you. Your honesty is refreshing." Then his grin disappeared and his brows pulled together. "I've got this thing on Friday night. It's a rodeo dinner that I have to attend. Would you join me as my date?"

His date? Her dreams were finally coming true. But was it years too late? She gulped down air. The sound wasn't sexy or feminine. Good thing the pale light hid the flush of color that was creeping up her face. Casey kept his eyes trained on her. She had to give him an answer. A dozen reasons to say no popped into her head. But how could she deny what she'd always wanted?

"I'd have to see if Mindy can watch Ally for a few hours but I would love to go."

He actually appeared relieved, as if he'd worried over her answer. "Good. It's black tie."

"Black tie?" A formal affair? Now she'd have to find something spectacular to wear on a budget. "Okay."

On Wednesday evening, Susanna stirred an enamel pot of bubbling chicken cacciatore. The pungent aroma of garlic and sweet onions filled the air. French bread was set out on the table, sliced and ready for buttering.

"Ally, will you please pick up the toys on the kitchen floor. Casey will be here for dinner any minute."

"Is Charger coming?" Ally asked. The raw hope in her voice sent Susie's heart spinning.

"Yes. Casey is bringing the puppy. He knows how much you love to play with him. Now put those things in your room, okay?"

"Oh, boy!"

Ally worked fast to clean up her mess and Susie moved to the sink to wash her hands. She turned on the faucet, and nothing happened. "What the…"

She moved the handle to the right. Water didn't flow. She turned it to the other side. No water flowed there either, not even a drip.

Her toes curled as beads of cold water seeped under her bare feet. She glanced down at the watery river surrounding her. "Oh, no." Bending, she yanked at the doors underneath the sink. The S-shaped formation of pipes grumbled and groaned. When she fell to her knees to get a better look, water suddenly squirted out, hitting her like a splash on a water slide. Her face, her blouse, her arms were all soaked. "Ugh!"

She backed away, struggling against the brute force. But the water kept coming. She had to dive in again. There was a knob toward the back of the space under the sink. If she could only get to it, she could shut the whole thing down.

She plunged forward, closing her eyes and reaching deep inside the cavity of the cabinet, desperately searching for the control valve.

"Move away, Susie. I've got this."

At that moment, she felt herself being guided back away from the surge of water. She opened her eyes and blinked.

Casey knelt next to her. His shirt was off and he was taking the pounding spray in the chest with much more finesse than she had. He reached in and with one try, managed to twist the knob that turned off the water, ending the leak that had drenched her.

Casey popped his head inside to inspect the pipes, then turned to her. "Are you all right?"

She did a quick sweep. She was soaked from head to toe but she wasn't hurt. "I'm fine."

Casey's eyes drifted down to her wet shirt and his eyes flickered over her breasts. Her taupe blouse did little to hide her reaction to the cold. "I'd be agreeing with you there," he said huskily.

Running her hands through her hair, she sat back and chuckled. She was beyond humiliated.

Casey laughed too, the warm and inviting sound helping her find some humor in this situation.

He sniffed the air. "Is something burning?"

"Oh, shoot! My cacciatore!" She rose quickly and instantly lost her footing on the slippery floor. She began to stumble backward. Casey moved into her path and reached out to catch her, bringing her tight against his bare chest. Only beads of moisture and a wet blouse separated them.

Oh, wow.

He didn't move.

Neither did she. It was like heaven being held by him. Seconds ticked by.

"Susie," he whispered, his mouth touching her hair. Goose bumps rose on her arms.

With his thumb, he tilted her chin and she peered into his deep azure eyes. The intensity burned straight through her.

Casey arched a brow and there was a low rumble in his throat. "One kiss," he said.

Then he dipped his mouth and claimed her lips.

It was more than a kiss. He devoured her, sweeping his tongue deep into the recesses of her mouth. She fought to breathe, to keep control of her senses. He cradled her face in his hands and the yearning inside her was unleashed. She was pulled into his magical spell.

From another room, her little girl's voice echoed in her head.

"Auntie? I put all my toys away."

Ally.

Casey pulled away immediately and reached for the shirt he'd flung onto the kitchen chair.

"That's g-good," she called out, watching him slip his arms into his sleeves and start buttoning up. She tossed him a dishtowel, which he caught with one hand and a grin. She used another one to wipe her face and blot her blouse. "I'm in the kitchen. Casey's here."

She turned to the oven to shut off the flame. The chicken had survived, barely.

Ally entered the kitchen and Casey walked over to her, casual as you please. "Hi, Ally."

"Hi."

"Charger's in the backyard. If your aunt says it's okay, we'll go outside and play with him in a little while."

Ally nodded, her blue eyes wandering over the flooded floor. "'Kay."

"We had a little leak, sweetie," Susanna managed to explain. The kitchen was a mess. And so were her nerves. Something special was happening between her and Casey and she wasn't sure what to make of it. Or whether she could trust what she was feeling.

"Susie, why don't you get cleaned up," he said, his gaze set firmly on her face. Heat climbed up her throat. She crossed her arms over her saturated blouse. Just a few seconds ago, they'd almost…she couldn't think about that now. "I'll keep an eye on Ally and clean up in here. I want to look at those pipes."

"What about you?" She pointed to where water was soaking through the button-down shirt he'd flung on in haste. His face was dotted with droplets.

"As soon as I'm through here, I'll get myself decent. Just grab some towels for the floor. Do you have any tools?"

"My dad's tools are in the garage. I'll get them."

He eyed her for a second, then nodded. "Thanks."

She should be thanking him. For fixing her leak. For catching her fall. For kissing her like his world revolved around her.

And all she had to offer him tonight was slightly scorched chicken cacciatore.

And a muffin.

The knock on Susanna's door came precisely at eight o'clock on Friday night.

How had she survived the week? She'd seen Casey nearly every day since Ally's birthday, whether he was fixing the plumbing or taking Ally for a walk with the pup or sharing a meal with them. Susanna just couldn't get away from him. She wasn't sure she wanted to. That was a revelation. She'd spent the last decade half in love with him, half hating him. Her brain didn't know what to think now, but oh, her heart said things that could get her into major trouble.

"He's here," she said to Mindy. She checked her appearance in the mirror, willing her nerves to settle down.

"Hang on a sec, hon."

"Why? Don't I look all right?"

She'd shopped this week for a new outfit, but nothing had jumped out at her and screamed PERFECT, so she'd opted for the meadow green lace dress she'd worn to her mother's wedding. It had a scoop neck with ruching around the waist and a skirt that reached the floor. She felt sort of like a fairy princess herself tonight.

"You look fabulous. That dress is killer, but don't be too anxious. Let him wait."

"Mindy, that's awful."

"Just looking out for my friend. What else can a prego like me look forward to, if not some juicy deets of your date."

Susanna shrugged. "I'm rusty when it comes to dating. There won't be much to tell."

She'd never dreamed she'd be dating Casey Thomas, not in a zillion years.

"Just remember, he asked you out," Mindy said. "The ball's in his court. You don't have to do a thing but sit back and enjoy the evening. Ally's already asleep, so it's all good. Have fun and don't worry about us."

"You're a good friend. This is a lot to ask of you." She hugged Mindy. "If you get tired or anything, or if Ally needs me, just call. You have my cell number and—"

"Go! Have fun. I'm disappearing."

Mindy waddle-walked down the hallway and once she was gone, Susanna glanced at the front door and tried to get her jitters under control. She'd never left Ally this long before. She didn't know what to expect from Casey. Why had she agreed to this?

Giving herself a mental pep talk, she grabbed hold of the knob and pulled it open.

Casey stood on her doorstep, his hands in the pants pockets of a jet-black tuxedo. She lifted her eyes to his ebony

Stetson. She hadn't seen him in one of those in years. It looked right on him. His roguish hair peeked out from beneath the brim. The whole cowboy tycoon package made her breathless.

"Damn," he said, whistling low, his gaze roving over her. "You look beautiful, Susanna."

"Thank you. You clean up pretty nice yourself."

"Thanks." His gaze flickered over her hair. She'd pulled it to one side with a rhinestone clip and curled the ends. With any luck the curls would hold for the entire night. "I like it."

She smiled. Where were her manners? "Would you like to come in for a little while? Ally's sleeping but if we're quiet…"

He stepped inside, and a hint of his cologne wafted to her nostrils as he walked past her. The lime and earth scent did things to her equilibrium every time. "Actually, the dinner starts in half an hour, so we should probably get going. Do you have a wrap?"

"It's right there." She pointed to her crepe shawl sitting on the entrance table. He retrieved it and she picked up her silver clutch purse.

He moved to her side with the shawl in his hand. "Do you want to wear it?"

"I don't think so. It's a warm night." Just looking at him in that tux heated her body through and through. She doubted she'd need the shawl at all.

"Ready to go then?" He opened the door. His hand found her lower back and he escorted her out the door. She locked up and almost did a double take when she turned and spotted a shiny onyx limousine parked in her driveway, a chauffeur standing at the ready, holding the door open for her. Her heart raced but her feet kept moving even when she wanted to come to a dead halt and ask Casey what was going on. He'd been mysterious about this date all week, giving her evasive answers when she'd wanted to know what the "rodeo thing" was all about.

She smiled and thanked the chauffeur, then slipped inside. Casey followed, as if he'd done this sort of thing a hundred times before. Susanna had never ridden in a limo. This was a first for her.

They backed out of the driveway and rode along the quiet streets. "I'm glad Mindy was able to watch Ally tonight," he said.

She nodded. "I'm nervous about it. I have my cell phone and gave poor Mindy a thousand instructions before I left."

Casey took her hand and placed it on his knee. She glanced at their joined hands. "She'll be fine. Chances are she won't ever know you were gone."

"I know all that, but it's such a big weight on my shoulders. It's more than a responsibility for me. I love her."

"She may call you auntie, but you're her mother now. I know she loves you too...who wouldn't?"

Susie's head snapped around and she was met with a sincere gleam in his eyes. A small smile wobbled on her lips. Did he see them quivering?

Casey leaned back in the seat and sighed, staring straight ahead. They remained with their hands entwined and speaking very little from then on. There seemed to be a new connection between them, something more powerful than she'd ever felt before. Was it due to the formal dress and privacy of the limo ride ? Or was it truly something else?

Something wondrous?

Casey hated these things. He didn't like attention poured over him and if it hadn't been for Austin and Elizabeth Brown insisting, he would've been glad to bypass this Think Pink Strong event. Every male in attendance at the Grand Palace Hotel ballroom was handed a pink ribbon to pin to his tuxedo lapel and every female was given a bud vase with a single rose. Subtle hues of carnation pink surrounded them from tablecloths to tinted wineglasses.

Susie was stunning tonight under sparkling chandelier light and Casey was glad he'd asked her to join him. She made the evening bearable. Hell, she made it downright enjoyable. He took her hand and led her to their round table at the front of the ballroom. Austin and Elizabeth Brown were already seated along with a few rodeo veterans Casey had come up the ranks with. Casey introduced Susanna to everyone and they took their seats.

"I'm so glad to meet you," Elizabeth said to Susie. Then the older woman turned to him and smiled. She'd already sized Susie up and decided she liked her. "I understand you and Casey are old neighbors."

"Yes, since childhood. Audrey is one of my best friends."

Austin put a hand on his shoulder. "I'm proud of Casey for the work he's done for Think Pink Strong. Ever since Elizabeth's recovery, Casey did his best to raise funds for breast cancer research. It's good that he's being honored tonight. Along with four other recipients, each one worthy."

Susie questioned him with her eyes. Then she picked up the program by her place setting. She read it like a speed reader and answered without missing a beat. "Yes, it seems his contributions to the cause have been extremely generous. He has a giving heart."

Flies didn't land on Susie. She caught on quickly and he was chewing himself out for not telling her about it earlier. Though, bragging rights over his charity work never did set well with him. He kept quiet about it mostly. And maybe he wanted Susie to accept his invitation for no other reason than she truly wanted to go out on a date with him.

"He never talks about it," Elizabeth said. "When we got wind of this dinner, Austin and I had to practically twist his arm to get him to accept his award tonight."

Thank you, Elizabeth.

He shrugged against Susie's stare. "I never expected an award."

"True, all the more reason you should be honored," Elizabeth said.

The waiters came by with piping hot sourdough rolls and the first course of spinach and prosciutto salad. Good thing, too: the subject of his fundraising was getting old.

Between courses, there were speeches and testimonials. Cancer survivors went up to the podium to tell their own stories of heartache and loss, as well as survival and hope. When Elizabeth had taken ill with the disease, Casey had known he wanted to help and he'd gotten involved raising funds using his rodeo fame for a good cause. It was something he believed in and pursued even after he'd broken his back.

After dinner, the award ceremony began and his name was announced. Susanna squeezed his hand and he felt all her warmth and encouragement in her touch. When he gazed into her eyes he found reassurance. He carried that with him as he walked up to the podium.

He wasn't good at making speeches, but this one came from the heart. He had a fondness for the Browns and he'd seen how helpless Austin had been when Elizabeth had had bad days. The cure had to be around the corner. If only he could be a small part of making that happen, he'd feel his purpose in life was somehow served.

As he accepted his award, he looked over at the Browns, who were listening to his words intently. Then his gaze drifted to Susanna. Her eyes had misted over and her smile rippled through his heart.

The other four recipients were called up to give speeches and afterward they were met with a rousing round of applause. Then Casey left the stage with his honoree plaque and returned to his seat, grateful the awards part of the evening was over. Austin rose to shake his hand and Elizabeth laid a kiss on his cheek, congratulating him. Orchestra music began playing and he didn't bother to sit. This was his chance to get Susie alone to explain. He leaned over to whisper in her ear, "Would you like to dance?"

Taking the napkin off her lap, she nodded and he extended his hand. She took it and he led her to the dance floor, then pulled her close the second their feet hit the parquet. He breathed in the scent of her hair, his nose deep in her shiny locks. Oh, man. The fragrance of vanilla filled his nostrils.

"Why is it so hard to accept recognition for the good you're doing?" she asked. But there was a glow in her eyes and softness in her tone. She wasn't angry with him.

"I don't do it for acclaim. I don't like receiving awards."

"Only championship buckles?"

He grinned. "Yeah, back in the day." He pulled her tighter in his arms. "I am glad you're here," he whispered in her ear. "Makes it easier."

"I'm glad I'm here too," she whispered back. "I wished you'd told me about this though."

He shrugged. "I guess I should have. The whole thing gives me hives."

She was impossible to resist, the prettiest woman in the room. He brushed her forehead with a soft kiss. His mind wasn't on charity tonight. It felt too damned good to dance with her, to have a legitimate excuse to hold her close. The lines of his mission here in Reno were blurring again. He'd helped Susie as much as she would allow and time was running short. He'd have to broach the subject of opening her own shop again, but not tonight. Tonight was about showing her a good time. Lord knew, she deserved it.

When the music ended, he wasn't ready to let her go. Another ballad began, a mellow tune that allowed him to hold her close again. He moved along with her, noticing the lightness in her steps, the softness surrounding her. Susie had always been a good kid, but now Casey thought of her as a woman, someone he couldn't get off his mind.

After a while, Austin cut in, whisking Susanna away, and Casey danced with Elizabeth. But Casey couldn't wait to get Susie back in his arms, which he did on the very next song. Four dances later, Susie waved her hand to fan her face. "Oh boy, I'm out of shape."

"No, you're not." She was…kinda perfect.

"I've never danced so much in my life."

"Are you having fun?"

"I am." Her eyes sparkled.

"Good." He glanced toward their table. "Looks like they're serving dessert and coffee now. You're saved." He grabbed her hand and led her back to the table.

Elizabeth and Austin had been eyeing him like two matchmaking hawks all evening. No doubt, they were curious about his date. While Austin had cut in to dance with Susie, he'd danced with Elizabeth and she'd quizzed him with a few subtle questions about his relationship with Susie. Hell, Casey had no real answers for her.

After dessert, the Browns stood to leave and while Elizabeth said farewell to Susie, Austin took him aside discreetly. "I like her." His expression held approval.

Casey blinked. "Don't get the wrong idea. We're just… friends."

Austin shook his head. "Don't go fooling yourself. You haven't taken your eyes off her all night. You were ready to punch me when I cut in on your dance."

Casey chuckled. "That's only because you have two left feet. I'm surprised you didn't break one of her toes."

"Laugh all you want, Casey. I know what I saw." His arms went around Casey's shoulders in a manly hug. "I'm proud of you, boy," he said, patting him on the back. "I'm glad we were here to see you honored."

The gap in his heart filled a little bit. He'd gone most of

his life without any kind of parental support and approval. Now, thanks to the Browns, he had a taste of what that was like. "I appreciate it. Means a lot to me to have you and Elizabeth here."

Next, he turned to say goodbye to Elizabeth, giving her a hug and kiss. The Browns joined the many other guests exiting the ballroom as the party wound down.

Casey snatched up Susie's wrap. "Time to go, Cinderella."

Susie rose from her seat and snickered. "If I'm Cinderella that would make you the handsome prince."

He had more than princely thoughts about her right now.

He laced their fingers. "If the shoe fits."

The sound of Susie's laughter stayed with him all the way to the limousine.

Eight

The air outside was heavy, though Susanna knew the air conditioner would be blowing briskly in the very private and contained backseat of the limousine. She got in, and Casey removed his jacket before joining her. As soon as the chauffer started the engine, Casey unfastened his tie, letting it hang loose around his neck, and unbuttoned the top three buttons on his shirt. She caught a moonlit glimpse of his chest again.

No wonder she couldn't breathe.

She'd seen him naked from the waist up briefly when her sink had decided to spring a leak. But it was different then. Ally was in the next room and, well, water was threatening to drown them both. But now, Casey's heat became her heat. And boy, was it stifling.

"Want a glass of champagne?" he asked, leaning forward to lift the bottle from the bucket of ice.

"Yes," she said. She wouldn't die happy if she didn't agree to sip champagne with Casey in the back of a limo. "Thanks."

He worked at the bottle and popped the cork, letting the bubbly spill over the rim. He captured most of it in a flute and continued pouring.

"You're good at that."

"One of my many talents." He smiled and handed her a glass, then poured one for himself. He touched the rim of his glass to hers. "To good causes."

"I like that." She lifted the flute to her lips and took a sip. The bubbles tickled all the way down in a light airy way that cooled her soaring temperature. "Mmm, that's good."

Casey's eyes gleamed as he watched her over his glass. She took a big swallow with trembling lips and gazed back at him. It was dark outside and only shallow light filtered into the limo. There wasn't really anywhere else to look but at his rugged, handsome face.

The bubbly liquor was going to her head as she noticed his gaze drifting down her chest. Her nipples hardened instantly from the sharp, hungry glint in his eyes.

"We'll be home in fifteen minutes," he said, clearing his throat. "Unless you want to take a drive for a little while."

She turned into a pumpkin at the stroke of midnight. It was before eleven and she also knew what going for a drive in this heated atmosphere meant. "A drive sounds nice."

Casey used the intercom to tell the driver the new plans. "Let's take a drive along the Truckee River."

Susanna sipped champagne until her flute was drained.

"Want another glass?" he asked, ready to quench her thirst.

"Not right now." There were enough dizzying thoughts making her head spin as it was.

Casey's beautiful mouth twisted in an awkward way as he returned the bottle to the bucket. "Now, that's too bad," he said, running his fingers along his chin.

"Why?" Had she done something wrong? She wasn't a saint, but she wasn't as worldly as the Lana Robardses of the world.

Casey took the empty glass from her hand and set it down. He leaned closer and whispered, "Because now I have no reason not to kiss you."

"Do you need a reason?" she blurted.

A devilish smile played across his lips. "Seems like lately, I've run out of reasons, doesn't it?" He touched a finger to her cheek and moved it slowly down to her mouth. That one simple touch sent her hormones flying. Her breath caught and froze in her throat as she waited...hoped.

He used his index finger to outline her upper lip, his roughened fingertip caressing over her softest flesh. She closed her eyes and parted for him. He bent his head to capture her mouth, clutching her around the waist, drawing her up close. She gasped from the shock of his heat and hunger.

His kisses were jarring. The impact thrilled her. Nothing she'd experienced before could top being with Casey in such close quarters, riding along streets she couldn't name, experiencing a lightness in her head and a heaviness that started in her breasts and dipped below her waist.

A groan sounded from deep inside his throat and he pulled her up onto his lap, taking advantage of the limousine's roominess to stretch out his long legs. He held her in his arms and eased her lower. She was completely at his mercy, her body lying across him, her gown hiked up and there was nowhere else on earth she'd rather be.

She'd fooled herself into thinking she wasn't in love with him. But now she knew how deep her feelings ran. The torch she'd carried for Casey all these years had only dimmed, but had never gone completely out. And now it was a bright fiery beacon, leading her to where she wanted to be all along. With him.

He smothered her with kisses and then moved his mouth down to the base of her throat, nibbling along her shoulder blade. Gently, he lifted the straps of her gown, shoving them down on her arms. The material gave way, and warm sultry air hit her chest. He kissed the soft swells of her breasts, his lips reverent and needy. She arched her back, aching for him to suckle, to claim her. And as he did, her nipples tightened to rounded beads that got harder with each moist stroke, each unbelievable lick of his tongue. Her body pulsed, jumping with electrifying pleasure.

"Ohhh," she breathed out.

She grew damp between the legs.

It was good, so good.

"You're amazing," he rasped between kisses.

His chest heaved up and down. All that power and heat being unleashed was a beautiful thing.

"I want you, sweetheart," he whispered, fanning hot breath over her chest. Her nipples strained and tightened even more. The air was thick and intense around her.

"I want you too, Casey."

He brought his mouth to hers and claimed her again and again. "Are you sure?"

"Yes," she whispered quickly. She rose up a little and hastily unfastened the rest of the buttons on his shirt. With his help, she removed it, and her lips immediately went to his chest. She kissed him there, her tongue roving over the incredibly hard smooth surface above his ribs. Susanna couldn't get enough of the taste of him mingled with the earthy subtleness of his cologne.

He roughly wove his fingers through her hair as growls of immense pleasure rose up from his throat. Then he slid his hands farther down to grasp the zipper of her dress. The metal teeth separated with a whisper and the material of her bodice fell away. He helped wiggle her out of the garment and it flowed onto the floor, draping partly over the champagne bucket.

Appreciation gleamed in his eyes as he gave her body a long look. "Beautiful, Susie."

She blushed and he smiled. Then he positioned her over his lap again and she felt the full force of his arousal. She moaned and he kissed her, his hand coming around to unhook her bra. Free of her restraint, her breasts jiggled and

Casey took one in his hand weighing the swell and lifted it to his mouth to suckle.

"Casey," she moaned. Electrical jolts rippled through her body.

Casey slipped one hand down past her navel and stroked over her panties several times, making her bite her lip to keep from screaming out as the pressure began to build.

It was torture and pleasure rolled up into one. Being naked in the limo with Casey was by far the most erotic thing she'd ever done. His fingers probed beneath her panties and he caressed and explored her most sensitive spot. Too soon, she splintered from his touch, her body wracked with lightning-like pulses that seized up and then shattered. Soft cries blew from her lips, her exquisite release a sweet hum singing through her body.

"Oh man, Susie," Casey was saying.

She gazed into his eyes and saw steam and raw sex there. "I want more," she said on a breath.

"Don't you worry, sweetheart. We're not through yet." Casey slid down and stretched his body out, taking up the entire length of the leather seat. He reached for her again, pulling her on top of him.

And within a minute, her panties were off, his zipper was down and he was sheathed in a condom that appeared just in the nick of time. He pulled her down to claim her lips in a deep, soul-rattling kiss. Then he lifted her up and adjusted her onto him. She uttered a low satisfied sigh as he buried himself in her.

Memories flashed of her first time with him. How she'd hidden the pain caused by his thrusts, how she'd pretended to know what she was doing. Not that she was an expert now—she'd had some experiences. But nothing compared to being joined with Casey tonight. Nothing.

She rode him, finding a special rhythm that satisfied them both. He plopped his Stetson on her head and grinned as they moved together. She only imagined how she looked, buck naked but for his hat and her three inch heels. And then the smiles were wiped off their faces, as his thrusts grew stronger, more forceful. She felt his body seize up. Hers did the same. It was rough and wild and amazing as they bucked and grunted together. "Susie," he hissed between his teeth.

She quickly joined him in his forceful release. Every cell in her body rejoiced. There were no words to describe the wonder. She only felt, experienced, enjoyed…and loved.

She fell on him, beads of her sweat mingling with his. He wrapped his arms around her and held her close, her body flush against him. She could stay like this forever, but reality called. She had no idea of the time, but it had to be late. She rose up and fought to free herself from Casey's strong arms. She hated to pull away from him, but she really did turn into a pumpkin when midnight struck. He rose to a sitting position next to her.

"Are you okay?"

She nodded, still too overcome to speak as she reached for her gown and covered herself with it.

He kissed her soundly on the lips and that righted her world. "We should probably get you home."

She nodded again. "Yes."

He gave instructions to the driver, and Susie knew despite the fully insulated privacy partition and tinted windows, she wouldn't be able to look the chauffeur in the eyes when she stepped out of the limo.

Casey helped her struggle into her dress. It had come off much more easily. And he put himself back together as well, buttoning his shirt and running a hand through his hair. Reaching for her, he brought her into the circle of his arms as the limo rolled toward home. She laid her head on his chest and closed her eyes. He brushed a kiss to her forehead and his lips lingered there.

Her heart tripped over itself. She'd never been happier.

Too soon, her fairy-tale carriage came to a stop. "Home," Casey said quietly.

He seemed reluctant to let her go, but as soon as the driver opened the door, Casey guided her outside and she made herself busy with her purse and wrap. Casey put his arm around her waist, thanked the driver and walked her to the door.

"Home before midnight," he said, eyes twinkling. "It was an amazing night."

She peered at him and nodded. "It was…" She squeezed her eyes closed briefly. "I don't usually do…what I mean to say is… I don't have—"

He put his finger to her lips. "Shh. Susie, I know."

How could he possibly know she didn't sleep around? Every time she'd really been alone with him, she'd let loose and they'd had sex. Well, okay…it had only happened twice, but in his eyes, he might look at her and see a different woman than the one she really was. "*How* do you know?"

"Because I know who you are."

His faith warmed her heart. But then thoughts of him with other women ran rampant in her mind. Did he wine and dine them and then make love to them in the backseat of a limo? Was that who Casey was? Maybe in his groupie rodeo days? Or maybe not. Susanna had never discussed his love life with his sister. Audrey said Casey kept his relationships to himself while he was raising her. Knowing how Casey had babied and protected Audrey, it made perfect sense.

"I only seem to lose my head around you," she confessed.

Casey planted a chaste kiss on her lips. "That makes me happy to hear."

"It does?"

He nodded, furrowing his brows. "Sure. Why wouldn't I want to hear that?"

"B-because the last time, you told me I was too young, we were neighbors and I was your sister's best friend. You told me it was a mistake."

"You mean ten years ago? When you were a teenager going off to college? Look, I know I could've handled it better back then, but all those things were true."

"And now it's different?"

He paused, his eyes flickering as if warring thoughts battled in his head. His expression worried her and assurances she hoped to hear didn't come. Instead Casey looped his arms around her waist and tucked her head under his chin. The heat of his skin seeped through his shirt and radiated out to her, yet he kept silent.

"Casey?"

"I don't have all the answers, Suse."

Susanna pulled back, her eyes snapping to his, her heart hammering against her chest. "What are you saying?"

The muscles in his jaw tightened. He seemed hard-pressed to get any words out. After a few seconds, he said, "That you're a wonderful woman and I want to spend more time with you."

Her shoulders relaxed. She didn't need a second to think about it. "I'd like that too." Casey Thomas was her ideal man. She wanted him like crazy.

She put her palms on his chest and eased them up to wrap her arms around his neck. Lacing her fingers, she gazed into his eyes. Sincerity reflected back at her and she knew he wasn't giving her a line. He meant every word. She had to trust in that. There was too much at stake. Ally's sweet face came to mind. She couldn't fall into something that would set Ally back or devastate her.

She didn't know when she'd be able to touch Casey like

this again. She savored every inch of him and when his lips came down on her she returned his kiss with everything she had inside.

On Saturday afternoon, Susie was right on time delivering the order for Joanna Picorelli's sweet sixteen chocolate party. With Ally as a helper, she set up her pastries on three separate tiered tables dressed with snowy white tablecloths and flower petals. It was a spread that would impress any connoisseur of fine chocolate, with her decadent devil's food double chocolate cupcakes, homemade chocolate raspberry truffles and cheesecake brownies.

Too excited after her date with Casey, Susie had woken up extra early and spent that time making sure she had everything perfect for the party. As Ally slept, she'd baked happily and rehashed her wonderful date with Casey. She should have been exhausted, yet her spirits were buoyed. She was almost afraid to give in to her feelings of love, but it was too late to go back.

She did feel a little guilty about fibbing to Mindy. "Casey won an impressive award for his fundraising and charitable contributions and we danced a little. Nothing happened," she'd said, with a shrug.

Poor Mindy. She'd looked so disappointed there wasn't something juicy going on. If she only had known that her friend had been initiated in the art of limo lovemaking, she might have gone right into early labor.

When Susanna was done setting up for the party, she drove straight home and parked in the garage. Ally was rubbing her eyes as they made their way into the house. Nap time called and after Susanna handed Ally a cup of grape juice, she scooted her into the bedroom. Ally chose five books from her shelf and Susie lay down on the bed with her. She began reading the first book quietly. Halfway through *Amelia Bedelia*, Ally's eyes shuttered closed. Susanna stayed with her a few minutes, catching some zees herself. A short time later, and careful not to make a sound, she tiptoed out of the room.

A flowery fragrance flavored the air as she moved down the hallway. She smiled and walked into the kitchen to give the bouquet Casey sent her this morning one more look. One dozen white lilies surrounded by greenery sat in a cut crystal vase on her kitchen table. When they were delivered she'd been surprised and thrilled. The note simply said, "For you to enjoy, Casey."

She took a seat and sighed, staring at the winsome flowers. For a few moments last night, after they'd made love, Casey's demeanor had changed. He'd been so deep in thought and tight-lipped that she wondered if he was regretting the entire evening. But then the flowers arrived this morning and her fears were put to rest. Somewhat.

Her phone rang and she caught it after the first ring, smiling when she noted the caller. "Hi, Mom."

"Hi, Susie…how are you today, honey?"

"Everything's great here. It's been *busy*, in a good way. How's Chip?"

"Oh, well…you know, he'd be better if his mother hadn't taken ill. Ida is ninety-one now. We've been spending a lot of time with her, making sure she's comfortable. That's the main reason I haven't come out to see you and Ally. Otherwise, you know I'd be there. I've been wanting to come for a visit for a while now."

"I can't wait for you to visit, Mom. But I understand. Chip needs you there now."

"You know, honey, our door's always open to you and Ally, if you'd ever consider moving here. I think you'd like Georgia and Chip and I would help you with that little shop you want to open."

"Thanks, Mom. I know your door is always open for us." She stared at Casey's flowers and couldn't hide the smile in her voice. "But I'm fine. Really. Aside from missing you, I'm happy here. Honestly, so you don't have to worry."

"Susie, honey…you know mothers always worry."

Susie chuckled. "I'm finding that out."

"And how's our little angel doing?"

Susie gave her mother the scoop about Ally's progress. She talked about the chocolate party she'd just catered and how things were starting to gel as far as motherhood and her business were concerned. Then she casually mentioned that Casey was coming over for dinner tonight.

"So how is Casey these days?" her mother asked.

"He's…fine."

"I always knew he was *fine*."

"Mother!"

"Well, you can't tell me you didn't have a crush on that boy when you were younger. You'd get tongue-tied whenever he came over. Your dad and I would have a good chuckle over it. Seems like you've been seeing a lot of him lately."

"He lives next door. Of course I see him. As much as I see any other neighbor."

It was a little white lie she couldn't avoid. Whatever was happening between her and Casey was too new to discuss with her mother right now.

Her mother's soft sigh reached her ears. "Well, you give that boy my best when you see him."

"I'll be sure to. Love you, Mom."

"Love you too."

"I'll call you in a few days."

"Okay, honey. And sweetheart…" Her mother paused for a second. "I don't know…you sound very happy today. It's good to hear."

"I am happy, Mom. Bye now."

Susie hit End and set her cell phone aside.

* * *

Standing at the threshold of Ally's bedroom, Susanna studied the little girl. All tucked in for the night, she looked adorable in her lightweight teddy bear PJs. Charger sound asleep beside her, his small furry chest puffing out noisy breaths. Ally had worn the puppy out and vice versa. Her heart swelled seeing the two of them looking like something out of a Norman Rockwell painting. But in that joy, she found room for fear. The psychologist had warned her to be cautious about upsetting any routine Ally had come to know. No big changes. No more devastation in her young life. How could she guarantee that?

A voice in her head told her to tread carefully...she was heading for uncharted territory with Casey. She closed the door partway and walked into the kitchen.

"Is she asleep?" Casey asked, greeting her in the middle of the room.

"Yes, thanks to you and Charger. I don't know which one of you three had more fun tonight."

Casey grinned. "Definitely me."

He looped his arms around her and kissed her tenderly on the lips. "Been wanting to do that all night."

"Mmm," she said. "I've been wanting you to do that all night."

Casey entwined their fingers and led her out of the kitchen. "Where are we going?"

"In here," he said. He sank down on her living room sofa and gave her hand a tug. *Whoosh.* She plopped onto his lap.

"Casey!"

"I have to thank you properly for dinner."

He took her in a long, slow, leisurely kiss.

"And I have to thank you for the beautiful flowers."

She returned his kiss, sucking on his lip as she pulled away. "There."

He brought his hands to her hair, toying with the curling ends. She loved the ease with which he touched her. They'd come so far in such a short time. "I've been thinking," he said. "About Sweet Susie's."

"That would be me."

"No," he said quietly. "I was talking about your shop."

"Oh." Where was this conversation heading? "I don't have a shop. Right now, I am Sweet Susie."

He cupped her neck and brought her head down for another kiss. "I won't argue with you there. But I was talking about you opening Sweet Susie's Pastries and More."

"It's not going to happen anytime soon, Casey." Her voice faltered. "I've sort of resigned myself to that."

"Don't you want it to happen?"

"More than anything." Well, almost. Right now, she had Casey on the brain. "I can't get the loan I need. And without that…"

"What if…and I'm just speculating here…what if I were to become your silent partner?"

She climbed off his lap to look at him and gain some perspective. "What do you mean?"

"I mean…what if I put up the money for Sweet Susie's. That place by the River Walk is—"

"Probably sold by now."

"You're right. It is sold. I bought it."

"What?"

"It's a great location."

"You bought it?" Had she heard right?

"Yeah. So if you want to give it a go…I'll back you."

Susie saw the sincerity and determination in his eyes. The implications went beyond business. Casey didn't need to partner with her; he ran a multi-million dollar business of his own. Was he pitying her, thinking of her as a charity case, or did he really care about her? This gesture was big and went way beyond sending her a bouquet of lilies. "I don't know…" Her voice trailed off.

"You don't have to make the decision now, Suse. Think about it and let me know when you're ready. There's no pressure."

"Okay," she muttered, still stunned.

He played with the scoop neck of her blouse, his index finger tracing along the seamless rim and his palm gently grazing her breast. "I should go," he whispered.

"Is that what you want?" she asked on a breath.

Casey paused, searching her eyes for a long moment. Again, something she couldn't name lingered in his expression. She couldn't read him, or know exactly what he was feeling. But she knew what she wanted. Him.

"Stay with me tonight," she offered.

Casey drew breath into his lungs. And then finally he nodded, any reluctance he might have felt wiped clean by a lopsided smile. "It would've been damn hard leaving you tonight."

She rose and put out her hand. He stood, towering over her, and allowed her to lead him into her bedroom.

As they entered the room, Casey closed the door with care and pressed the button lock. "Okay?" he whispered.

Lifting her eyes to his, she nodded. Ally was sound asleep, but just in case, she didn't want her wandering into her bedroom tonight and Casey understood that. Susie had eagle ears and she'd hear Ally if she needed her.

The air was warm in her room, the silence rich with tension. Casey grasped her hand and moved toward the queen-size bed. With a sudden yank, he dragged her to his chest and his lips whispered over her ear, "Finally, I'll make love to you in a bed."

Their time on the sofa when she was eighteen held special memories, and so did the limo ride—she'd never forget either night. "I'm not complaining," she said softly.

"You deserve…more, Susanna," he rasped in a low tone. "You deserve everything."

"Oh, Casey," she crooned, her heart swelling. She brought her palm to his stubbly cheek, loving this rugged side of him. "I think I have that right now."

"I don't know about that."

She'd had reservations about Casey in the beginning, but things were changing between them. He'd been there for her at every turn lately. If she didn't go for this chance with Casey and see where it all might lead, she'd never forgive herself. She trusted her feelings for him that much. Otherwise, she'd never risk her heart. "But *I* know. I want you here tonight. That's all that matters."

She rose up on tiptoes and kissed his lips.

A groan rose from his throat and he lifted her into his arms, caveman-style, holding her there while he answered her kiss with a dozen of his own. Then he lowered her down on the bed and simply stared at her as she stretched out and nuzzled her head into the pillow. Her hair fanned out, catching his rapt attention. The bed dipped as he placed a knee by her hip and then pushed her Sweet Susie's T-shirt up, his fingers inching up her sides, his eyes focused on their path. The material hooked onto her breasts and he used enough gentle force to slip it up and over. Staring down at her, he said, "I didn't think it could get any better."

He stood up and lifted his polo shirt over his head. Next, he unbuckled and removed his belt. Susie took in the play of moonlight on all that lean muscle. She'd never tire of seeing Casey this way, half naked, his eyes lit with pure lust.

Oh, boy.

He lowered down beside her and resumed their kiss. Her skin prickled as he caressed the hidden places of her body. She was his now, she knew. She wouldn't question anything he did to her. Anything he took. She loved him from the depths of her soul. Lying with him on the bed made it all seem more real somehow, made it all seem right.

He kissed her lazily, as if he had all the time in the world. He touched her thoroughly, everywhere, and she moaned and arched her body, straining to be closer to him. His mouth covered one breast and suckled while his hand toyed with her upper thighs. Anticipation grew fiery hot, her breaths came up short. He separated her legs and she waited. "Casey," she moaned. Her body stilled, ready.

"Shh, sweetheart," he said. "I want to make it good for you."

How could it get any better?

Another round of his kisses bruised her lips, and then… he moved down her body and tasted her, his tongue moistening her most sensitive spot, his day-old beard chafing her soft inner thighs. Sensations whipped through her. A scream rose up, threatening to break through the quiet, and instantly, as if he anticipated her reaction, his hand was there, covering her mouth, his firm fingertips muting her sounds. Forced into heady silence, she calmed and enjoyed the rippling tremors bounding through her system with every beat of her heart.

Her powerful and earth-shattering release came quickly, her heart racing like mad.

"Good?"

"So…good," she said on a quiet sigh.

Then Casey quickly put on a condom and positioned himself over her, his arms braced on the bed by her pillow. A sheet of blond hair hid his handsome face, but she saw the tilt of his rigid jaw and felt his body tighten. "Ready for me?" he asked.

She always had been.

She nodded. "Oh, yes," she whimpered. "Please."

He inhaled a sharp breath and mounted her.

It was perfect, the patient rhythm he set. His slow thrusts

repeatedly brought her to the brink. He stroked her body over and over, and whispered in her ear, "Again, sweetheart."

The sexy words tilted her world upside down. She went instantly tight. Her body bucked up and convulsed. Casey drove deeper, climbed higher. Her name tore from his lips and she couldn't hold on a second longer. She climaxed, splintering into a thousand embers of fiery heat.

With a low, deep guttural sound, Casey gave one more thrust, shuddering over her. He stilled then and exhaled. They stayed together like that for quiet seconds, with him over her, staring into each other's eyes, breathing and allowing their bodies to simmer. Then Casey rolled off and lay on the bed beside her. He slipped his arm over her shoulder and she closed her eyes.

She was in Casey heaven.

Susanna lay nestled in Casey's arms, her head on his chest and wisps of her hair tickling his chin. Gently, he glided his fingertips over her arm, soaking up the softness of her skin in the aftermath of making love. She smelled deliciously sweet like the cupcakes she baked and he'd never tire of breathing in her scent. Susie had grown into a wonderful woman, a caring mother and a responsive bed partner.

His mission here had been complicated from the start. He'd had to gain Susie's trust and insinuate himself into her life, in order to give her a hand up without her realizing it. He was succeeding in that, for the most part. But he'd never planned on falling for her. He'd never planned on caring so darn much for her and the little child she was raising.

Susanna Hart was a woman he could spend his life with and not ever look back. Because there was a child involved and because he didn't want to hurt Susie again, he had to tread carefully. He couldn't afford any mistakes this time.

He wanted Susie and at the moment, as her warm breath touched his skin, he saw nothing but possibilities with her. Was it wishful thinking? He wasn't sure, but one day soon he'd tell her the truth about himself and own up to his reason for coming here. But right now, he held onto his secret. Right now, he couldn't risk failing in his mission.

Right now, he wasn't ready to risk it all.

"Mmm, Casey," Susanna purred, shifting her body closer, getting more comfortable on his chest. "This is nice."

He began stroking her hair, his palm caressing the silky locks as soft sounds of satisfaction slipped from her throat. He'd never enjoyed snuggling with a woman like this before. "It's the very best."

Nine

Susanna held a vigil by her kitchen window, glimpsing Casey taking his morning run as she had almost every single day since he'd moved in next door. It made her day, seeing him pounding pavement in gray sweats, a white tank and beads of sweat coating his shoulders and arms. Charger kept pace beside him, panting and going as fast as his stubby legs allowed. Her eyes followed Casey until her view was blocked by Mrs. Simpson's shady oak tree. In about twenty minutes, and if she was lucky, she'd see him return to Meadow Drive, slowing his movements to walk off the burn.

Oh, she missed him already.

It was the same every morning when she'd wake up alone in bed after spending an exhausting and beautiful night with him. If he suspected she was beat, he'd leave before midnight, and if time got away from them, he'd hold her in his arms while they both slept and leave sometime during the wee hours of the morning before her alarm went off.

The week had flown by. She couldn't believe it was Saturday already and time for the grand opening of Zane's on the River. She wanted to look extra special for Casey tonight. And she'd recruited Mindy for the job. While she looked forward to her second official date with Casey, the opening of the restaurant and nailing down a new office site meant that his job here was almost completed.

A headache suddenly pounded inside her skull. The unknown frightened her. This week she'd lived in the moment with Casey. Although he didn't make any verbal promises, his kisses did a lot of talking. Had she misread him? And the kindness he'd bestowed on her and Ally lately?

Last Monday, she'd found him directing a workman he'd employed to fix their adjoining backyard fences. On Tuesday, a painting crew splashed a new coat of paint on her sun-bleached patio cover after they'd done a touch up job at the Thomas house. Wednesday brought a gardener who planted feathery snow-white iceberg roses and greenery in the garden border by her front porch. Casey said he wanted to give her flowers that would last. She could hardly refuse.

Yesterday morning, though his back was hurting despite the rubdown she'd given him the night before, he'd taken Ally on a walk with Charger so Susie could complete a big order. Ally had been thrilled. Casey was one of her favorite people. And she was over the moon about the puppy.

"Remember, Charger's only here for a short time, Ally. He'll be leaving one day," she would gently warn her.

She should be giving herself the same warning about Casey.

After watching him finish his cooldown and go back inside his house, Susie went about her morning rituals, baking and delivering her goods with Ally by her side. In the afternoon, Mindy came over and Susie drove the three of them to the mall. While Ally climbed the rungs of the slide ladder at the indoor playground, Mindy and Susie finished their curry chicken salads at a café table just steps away. Susie kept her eyes on her charge. Ally grabbed the plastic sides of the slide and enjoyed the ride all the way down.

When her feet hit the ground, she bounded up. "Lookee, auntie. I did it!"

"I see that, Ally. Good girl!"

Other children joined in and Ally got in line to climb up the slide again.

"This is amazing," Susie said to Mindy, lifting the last forkful of salad to her mouth. She rarely had time to take Ally anywhere fun and eat out.

"What's amazing is how you can keep a secret from me for so long." Mindy's voice lowered and she glanced around before giving her a direct look. Susie released a sigh. *Here it comes.* "You're dating Casey Thomas."

"You already know that. You agreed to watch Ally again tonight. I promise this is the last time I'll ask."

"I hope it's not. And what's really going on between you two?" Mindy sipped her lemonade, eyeing her thoughtfully over the glass. "You have to give me something."

"Okay, so maybe…" Susie took a deep breath. Admitting their sort of relationship out loud meant truly owning up to it. Until now, the secret wedged into her heart was private and protected. "Maybe…we've spent a few nights together."

Mindy's mouth gaped open.

"You're gonna catch a fly that way."

Mindy clamped her mouth shut.

"It's…it's…" Susie shrugged a shoulder. "I don't know what it is."

"You're having sex with him?"

"Shh…" She glanced at Ally. She'd made a friend and they were taking turns on the slide and chattering. How sweet. "Yes, okay," she admitted.

"Wow!" Mindy's eyes beamed.

"Wow is right." She blushed.

"Oh Suse…I'm stunned. I'm happy for you, too. I mean, Casey's hot."

"I know."

Casey was much more than hot. He'd been a friend to her first, even when she didn't want him to be. And he'd been around a lot. Whether he knew it or not, he was making life easier for her. How could she possibly not love him?

"You're wild about him, aren't you?"

There was no point lying. Mindy would see right through her. She nodded.

Her friend reached out for her, touching her wrist and squeezing. "Oh, honey. I'm glad you found someone, but be careful."

"I will. I am." She fibbed. She was trying to be cautious, but her emotions were already too far gone.

"Okay. Just looking out for you." Mindy's hand rested on her melon belly. A pregnancy glow glistened on her face and her almond-shaped brown eyes twinkled.

"You're a good friend, Mindy. Thanks for not judging me."

"There's nothing to judge. I say go for it, if he's the guy you want."

"He is."

"Well, then we have a clear mission. We are going to find you the perfect dress for your hot and heavy date with breathtaking Casey Thomas."

"You look gorgeous tonight, Susie." Her skin prickled as Casey's gaze traveled over her daring black dress made of form-fitting, marshmallow-soft leather and delicate lace. He offered her his hand and she slipped out of his Cadillac SUV gracefully, praying she wouldn't trip on her short boot heels.

"I hoped you'd like it." Mindy had insisted that basic black was the way to go and when they'd found the dress in a fashionable boutique at the mall, it was a must-buy. It was worth dipping into her savings to impress Casey. He'd done a whole of lot of impressing her lately—in and out of bed.

She giggled out loud and then caught herself.

"Something funny, sweetheart?"

She had a secret lover and it was the one man she'd always wanted. How lucky was she? "No, I'm just a little giddy."

"Giddy?"

She met his eyes and saw something bright and beautiful in them.

Casey's lips twisted. "Oh, I'm getting the picture. It's because you're having dinner with the super talented Zane Williams tonight."

"Maybe I'm giddy for a different reason." She smoothed out his raven-black dinner jacket and then straightened his collar.

"Oh, yeah?" He lowered his head toward her and his arms came around her waist. Gently, he drew her to his chest. They stood on the sidewalk beside the lush, landscaped gardens leading to the restaurant. He didn't seem to mind who saw them acting like hormonal teens. His warm lips came down on hers and an impatient sound rose from his throat. After the kiss, he nuzzled her hair and sighed. "Oh, man. In another minute, I'm gonna have to dunk myself in that doggone river," he whispered.

Susie giggled again and he gave her a warning look. Taking her shoulder, he turned her to face the restaurant. "What do you think?"

Festive bubble lights illuminated the grounds, highlighting the private, invitation-only grand opening gala of Zane's on the River. The stone masonry and wood beam architecture was exquisite. The building itself was an equal compilation of modern and rustic with the second story bay windows surrounding the structure acting like skylights. The double doors were heavy and carved with layers of beveling. "It's stunning, Casey. You should be proud."

He nodded, gleaming with pride. "Thank you."

Casey had come a long way and she was struck by his success. He didn't let his injury get him down. He'd moved on with his life and risked a great deal to become CEO of Sentinel.

Grabbing her hand, he led her through the doors and into the restaurant. "Zane doesn't appreciate swooners," he said into her ear.

She doubted that. Zane's husky voice and antics on stage were designed to make women lightheaded. At the one concert she'd attended, she witnessed a young girl faint dead away. Poor thing had to be revived with smelling salts. The paramedics had carted her off and she never did get to see the rest of the concert. "I'll try to remember that."

A quiet snort of laughter rose from his throat and he grinned.

The hostess showed them to their table. And shortly afterward, Zane Williams entered the restaurant. His six-foot-two frame, black hat and charming superstar smile commanded attention. He knew how to handle fame. He accepted it with grace and his fans appreciated his down-to-earth attitude. She watched him shake hands with his guests and thank them for coming. Susie looked around at the attractive women and well-groomed men in attendance. Tonight, she was mingling with A-list peeps.

Zane finally made his way toward them and sat down next to her. Her heart pounding, she slid a glance at Casey and he winked.

"Hello, darlin'. Susanna, right? Did you bring me one of those delicious muffins?"

Gosh, he remembered her name. "No…but I'll make sure to get some to you."

"I'm just funning you, but dang it…I wouldn't complain if a batch landed on my doorstep one morning." His jacket brushed her shoulder when he reached over to shake Casey's hand. "Good to see you, man."

"Same here, Zane. And mind your manners with my date."

Susanna's breath caught. Had Casey really said that? Surely, Zane Williams wasn't flirting with her.

"So, you're dating now." Zane leaned his elbows on the table and hunkered down. "Finally Casey's showing some smarts in the female department. I could tell you stories...."

"She doesn't want to hear them," Casey drawled. "And that subject is forever closed."

Susie blushed. It wasn't every day she was the topic of conversation with a country superstar. But she liked hearing Casey call her his date, even if it was competitive banter between two strong men.

"My lips are sealed," Zane said. He wore dark slacks and a tastefully decorated studded shirt, nothing too flashy, but his wardrobe definitely set him apart from the crowd. "So the manager, Toby, says they'll be ladling up samples of our chef's favorites to every table. Hopefully, the food, the service and all will hit the mark."

A waiter came by to take drink orders. Zane and Casey ordered whiskey straight up and Susie requested a glass of white wine. After the drinks were delivered, a ruggedly handsome man joined their table; he had to be Zane's brother, the two looked so much alike. Another couple of men took their seats and introductions were made. Zane's brother Caleb asked everyone to call him C.W.

When everyone had settled in, appetizers were served. Susie took small bites of Thai shrimp over a bed of polenta. The Southwest Asian fusion dish tasted spicy and sweet. "I like it," she said.

Casey agreed, nodding his head. "Not half bad."

During dinner, Zane spoke to everyone at the table about his upcoming tour starting at the end of the month, which led to a lively conversation. The sampling of food was rich and delightful. There were a few dishes a little too out there for her taste buds, but overall Susie liked the fare.

Susie recognized members of Zane's band setting up on an elevated platform in a portion of the restaurant cleared of tables. There were a few strums of a guitar, a few beats on the drums and a grating screech of the microphone as the guys tuned up their instruments. Zane left the table to head up his band, grabbing the now-functioning mike.

"I apologize for the acoustics. This place wasn't exactly designed for this," he said. "But my band can make just about anything sound pretty good, including me." He chuckled and then looked out at the sixty or so people seated at tables in the softly lit room. "First of all, I want to thank all of you, my friends, for coming out to taste test our food and enjoy the restaurant. I'm pretty doggone proud of the way this place turned out. Now, if you'll allow me," he said, "while I have you at my mercy, I think I'll try out a few new songs on you…and maybe some old ones too."

Casey put his arm along Susie's chair and dropped his hand possessively onto her shoulder. The lights dimmed everywhere but where Zane was standing. Casey leaned close, his breath fanning her cheek. Then his lips were brushing over hers softly, tenderly. The short sweet kiss touched her heart in too many ways to name. Tender emotions welled up. Could a person die from too much happiness?

The first songs were new, upbeat tunes that Zane had written himself. Susie, along with just about everyone else in the room, tapped her feet and clapped her hands to the music.

Applause broke out when he stopped singing and the room quieted again when Zane grabbed a bar stool and sat down, slipping his guitar strap over his head. "You all come up here now and dance. I'm singing a ballad this time, guys, so no excuses about having chicken legs. Take up your girl, and come onto the floor." Zane aimed a taunting look at their table. "That includes you, Casey."

Casey's immediate chuckle rang in her ears. He gave her shoulder a gentle squeeze. "Guess we've got no choice now. Dance with me?"

As if there was any chance she wouldn't. "If I have to," she said, smiling.

They rose and he led her to the dance floor. They fit together perfectly now, all awkwardness and reserve gone. Their arms and hands knew just where to go as they swayed to Zane's heart-wrenching tune of lost love. Casey whispered for her ears only, "No offense to Zane, but I can't wait to get you home."

"Mmm." She was being serenaded in an intimate concert by her favorite country idol and yet being home with Casey sounded so much better. She snuggled tighter in Casey's arms and he brushed a kiss to her forehead.

An hour later, she was in the car with Casey driving home, eager to be alone with him.

"Did you have fun tonight?" he asked, entwining their fingers and placing her hand on his leg.

She loved the little gestures that connected them. "I did. Sort of like a dream, amazing and lovely all at once."

"I could say the same about you." He glanced over. "Amazing and very lovely."

Her eyelids fluttered. "Thank you."

He reached around her neck and tugged her close. She leaned as far as the seat belt would allow and he darted a glance at the empty road, then turned his head and brought his mouth hungrily to hers. A blast of desire swept through her, hot and dangerous. The kiss ended and Casey leaned all the way back in his seat to stare at the road, huffing out a pent-up, frustrated sigh.

His cell phone rang. "Damn, who's calling me at this hour?" Casey glanced at his watch. Susie knew it was after eleven. He punched the Bluetooth button on his steering wheel. "Yeah?"

"Hey, Casey. It's Luke." His brother-in-law's tone immediately put a frown on Casey's face. "Sorry to call so late but—"

"What's wrong?" he demanded.

"It's Audrey. She's been doubled up in pain for hours. At first we thought it was food poisoning. She just kept heaving and I didn't like it. I rushed her to emergency. Oh, man…I'm so damn worried about her."

"What did they say? What's wrong with her?"

"They're prepping her for surgery now. It's her appendix."

"Ah, hell, Luke. Did it burst?"

"No, thank God. We caught it in time."

"Tell her I'm coming. Where are you?"

"Douglas County Hospital."

"Be there as soon as I can." He pushed the Off button and winced.

"Oh, no," Susie said, chewing her lip. She'd heard the entire conversation and the fear on Casey's face scared her. Her heart pounded hard against her chest. She hated the feeling of dread. It reminded her too much of when her father was ill. "Casey, I want to come with you, but Ally…"

"You can't leave Ally tonight. I know. It's too much to drag her out in the middle of the night."

"She doesn't like hospitals. She has bad memories of them because of her mom."

Casey nodded.

The drive home seemed to take an eon. When they finally pulled up to the house, Susie covered his hand. It was shaking. "Please be careful driving."

He nodded again. "Don't worry."

She swallowed past a lump in her throat. "When you

see Audrey, give her my love. I'm praying she's going to be okay."

"She will be," he said. But what Susanna really heard was, *she has to be.*

Casey sat in the hospital waiting room, slumped down, his legs stretched out and his eyes closed. His third cup of coffee had grown cold sitting in its cupholder on the arm of his chair. Audrey had come out of surgery just fine. Thank God, thank God. He'd never get over his protective instincts when it came to his sister. He'd had a lifetime of worrying over her. Even if they butted heads at times, he'd never protected anyone the way he had Audrey.

Luke was in with her now. She'd woken up an hour ago. Ava was in good hands with her Aunt Kat and Uncle Justin back at Sunset Ranch. Kat was a natural with babies. She'd raised Connor practically alone until Justin claimed him as his son. Luke's other brother, Logan, and his wife, Sophia, had been here, keeping Luke company until they were sure Audrey was out of danger.

Casey had gone in to see Audrey while she slept off the anesthesia. She hadn't known he was there or seen the tears welling up in his eyes as he looked upon her pale face.

"You can go in to see her now," Luke was saying. Casey's eyes snapped open. "Audrey's asking to see you."

Stiff in the joints, Casey rose and straightened his back out slowly. "Thanks. How is she?"

"She's a little groggy, but feels pretty good, considering. It was a close call. The surgeon said it was a good thing she got here when she did. The appendix was pretty close to bursting."

"Oh, man." He put his hand on Luke's back. "It's a good thing you insisted on bringing her in. Audrey never cooperated with me so much."

"Yeah, well. I played my trump card. I used Ava as a

weapon. Audrey would do anything for our little girl. Besides, the pain got so darn bad, she didn't have the strength to argue."

Casey's heart seized up. He hated thinking of his little sis in pain. "I'm going in to see her now. Why don't you go home and check on Ava."

"That's exactly what Audrey asked me to do. The doctor says she doesn't have to stay overnight, which is a good thing. Audrey misses Ava like crazy."

"Then go. I'll stay with her until you come back."

"Promise to call me if anything comes up."

"I will," Casey said. Then he walked down the hallway and into Audrey's room.

She had a big blurry-eyed smile for him. "Casey, hi." She was propped up in bed, wearing a green and white checkered hospital gown, her head supported by two stiff pillows. Her words came out slowly, her voice a little muffled. "You didn't have to come. You waited all night for me," she said.

"Yes, I did have to come. I had to make sure you were okay." He strolled over and kissed her on the forehead, letting his lips linger for a second as he squeezed his eyes shut. It was good to see her awake and out of danger, even if she was fog-brained at the moment.

"I have the best big brother," she whispered.

"You didn't say that while you were growing up."

Even in her half-drugged state, she rolled her eyes. "You've changed."

He laughed with relief, refusing to argue. "You gave us a big scare. Luke was going crazy."

"It was no walk in the park for me either, big brother. But I hated that Luke worried himself. I sure do love that man."

"Spare me."

His best friend had gotten his little sis pregnant and, stubborn as she was, she'd refused to marry him at first, despite Casey's demands and Luke's inept proposal.

He pulled up a chair by the side of her bed, turned it backwards and straddled it. "So you're feeling okay, really?"

"Ready to run a marathon today."

Casey studied her face. A flush of color replaced the ashen tones from earlier this morning. She was groggy from the meds, but Audrey's attitude seemed up to snuff. If she gave him sass, she was feeling pretty darned good.

"So the prognosis is good?"

"That's what the doctor says. They're letting me go home later today." Her eyes misted, a sudden gush of emotion spreading over her face. "I can't wait to see Ava. We've never been apart."

"You will." He took her hand to reassure her. "I bet Luke brings her to pick you up."

"Gosh, Casey. It's scary how much I love that little girl."

Casey used his other hand to rub the back of his neck. Thoughts of Susanna and Ally popped into his mind. More and more he was picturing himself with them now. And more and more, the blurry lines of that image were becoming clearer in his mind. Soon, he'd tell Susie the truth. "She's a sweetheart."

"Speaking of sweethearts, how's my friend S-Susanna and her little Ally? Are things going well…with our plan? We haven't spoken for a while."

The plan? Casey thought of Susie and Ally differently now. He hadn't thought of them as his mission lately. There was more to it than that. But no matter what happened in the future, he had managed to get some things accomplished and he felt damn good about that. "She sends her love, honey. And it's going well. Suse is thinking about opening her shop finally. I offered her a partnership."

"Suse?" Audrey's face softened and her mouthed slanted up. "Did you just call her Suse?"

Casey let her question roll off him. "She's got a good

head on her shoulders. She's going to give me her answer soon. She and Ally need some stability in their lives and the shop will give them that. She's doing a terrific job raising that little girl."

"I can't imagine raising Ava without Luke." Tilting her head, she spoke slowly. "I remember how we would spend our summers daydreaming about getting married and having babies. Susanna always wanted a big family of her own. I guess that comes from being an only child. We had baby names picked out and everything. Anyway," Audrey said, her soft voice whimsical now, "my fantasy life is coming true. I hope the same happens for Susanna one day."

Casey stared at his sister. A watery mist welled up in his eyes, making it hard to focus.

Audrey's words brought new meaning to heartache.

Susie always wanted a big family.

He felt the bitter acid rise in his gut and splash onto everything warm and happy inside him. He'd never felt more broken than right now. Split in half. The truth was his slayer and there was no way around the defeat.

Didn't Austin tell him he would've done things differently in his life so that Elizabeth could've had children? Didn't his mentor and good friend regret that he'd let his wife down? That he'd let growing his business dictate their lives, until it was too late for them to have children? He'd almost lost Elizabeth because of it.

Casey shuddered.

What was he thinking? He couldn't have Susanna. It wouldn't be fair to her. He couldn't give her what she wanted. She'd already made enough sacrifices in her life.

He loved her too much to allow her to make this sacrifice for him.

He loved her.

Hell, how could he be around Susie and *not* fall in love with her? True, in the beginning, he hadn't seen it coming, but as he got to know her, day in and day out, there seemed no way to shut down his emotions. They'd over-powered him.

Now, his heart ached in a way it never had before. And the sad reality was that he could never give Susanna the big family she wanted.

He didn't want Audrey to see him this way. Mustering a smile, he reassured her, "I'm...sure Susanna's life will turn out just fine."

"Casey, are you okay? Your face just turned sheet white."

He sighed and then lied to his sister. "That's what not eating or sleeping all night will do to you. I'm not as young as I used to be, kiddo."

Later that afternoon, Casey turned into the driveway of his Reno home with a lump in his throat. Charger came running off Susanna's porch, making a beeline for his car. Now, of all times, the dog was eager to see him? Susanna had kept him overnight while he visited his sister.

"Charger!" Susie's sweet voice rang in his ears. She came barreling off the steps, with Ally in her arms. His chest constricted seeing the two ladies in his life racing toward him, both giddy with laughter.

Susie wore her usual Sweet Susie's lavender T-shirt and a tight pair of studded blue jeans. Her hair was loose and flowing behind her in a wash of cinnamon curls. Ally waved to him. She looked adorable in a yellow gingham sundress, her blond locks lifted in two ribbon-encased pigtails.

He couldn't help smiling. They were magnificent.

His love for them poured over him in sudden unequivocal waves, a torrential rain that was unstoppable, and the pain it caused knotted his stomach and burned a hole in his heart.

He opened his car door and his boots hit asphalt as he

lumbered out. He slumped his shoulders, feeling weary and confused but straightened before Susie noticed. Shouldn't loving someone feel better than this?

Charger's scrappy paws were on his legs instantly; the little bundle of energy took Casey's mind off his problem. He lifted the puppy up and scratched him under his chin. The pup's tail whipped against his chest. "Easy now, Charger."

And then Susie was there, facing him. Ally smiled, giving him a little wave. "Hi."

"Hi," he said to her.

"I'm glad you're back," Susie said. Her face beamed and he wanted to return the joy, but said nothing.

"How's Audrey?" she asked, breathless.

"She's doing pretty well, considering what she went through. Luke's there with her now. With any luck, she'll be home before dark. She'll make a full recovery."

"That's a relief. I called the hospital a few hours ago to see if she could talk to me, but she was sleeping. I'm glad you called me this morning to give me an update."

"Sure, no problem. I was happy to do it." He put the dog down. "Thanks for watching the pup. I hope he wasn't too much trouble for you." He used a formal tone that had Susie blinking her eyes.

"Not at all." She studied him now.

Ally begged to be let down and Susie lowered her to the ground. "Stay close, Ally."

When she straightened, her eyes were two probes into his soul. "Anything wrong?"

He shrugged. "I'm just beat. It's been a long twenty-four hours. I think I'll hit the sack early."

Susie nodded. "Well, okay. If you want Charger out of your hair, I'll watch him again."

She already did too much. He wasn't going to pawn his dog off on her again. "No, that's not necessary, Susanna."

There was a note of longing in her eyes that seemed to equal his own. It took a great deal of willpower not to kiss her senseless and tell her what she meant to him. But it was better this way for her. He couldn't resume their relationship now or give her false hope. He had to tell her the truth and break it off with her.

"Well, then. Get some rest tonight, Casey."

"Will do," he said to her. Then he shifted toward the dog. "Charger! Come." He slapped his thigh and the pup's head popped up. He didn't waver this time. He left Ally's side, trotted over and they both entered the house together.

Casey walked straight into the kitchen, opened a cabinet and pulled out a bottle of Scotch and a shot glass. He carried them into the living room, turned on the television and sank down onto the sofa. But he didn't take a drink immediately. He sat up, braced his elbows on his knees, closed his eyes and covered his face with his hands. What now? This was all a big giant-size mess. There was only one way out. Tell Susanna the truth and be done with the agony.

Charger jumped up on the sofa, circled around a few times, then landed with his chin on Casey's lap. Absently, he stroked the dog's champagne coat and stared at the screen. A classic western was ending. The starch-shirted cowboy mounted a speckled pinto and reined the horse toward the blazing sunset, leaving the sweet-faced girl behind. Somehow, it seemed charming and romantic on the silver screen.

In real life?

Not so much.

Susie arranged pieces of southern fried chicken, mashed potatoes with gravy and honey corn muffins on a plate. Covering the dish with aluminum foil, she sealed the edges and reminded Ally, "Remember, we have to be really quiet, sweetie. Casey might be sleeping when we get over there."

She put the note she'd written on top of the covered dish. If Casey didn't answer his door, she planned to put his meal in his fridge, leave him the note and dash in and out of his house without waking him. Hooking his keychain on her finger, she grabbed the plate and extended her hand to Ally. "Let's go."

Ally thought it was all fun and games.

Susie hoped Casey would appreciate the gesture. He was a hopeless cook and if he woke up hungry, he'd have a nice meal waiting for him. All he'd have to do was microwave it.

She knocked softly on Casey's back door.

Silence answered her.

She knocked again, her ear close to the door. She heard no movement or sounds.

Charger was probably asleep too.

"Okay, Ally. Stay with me and don't say a word."

Tiptoeing into Casey's kitchen, just off the back doorway, Susie made her way toward the refrigerator. Ally was steps behind her, giggling quietly. Susie grinned. Luckily, Casey was a sound sleeper. She doubted Ally's soft noises would carry to his bedroom.

Susie enjoyed doing nice things for Casey. A meal here, a backrub there. It wasn't much but it was all she had to offer him. He'd been doing nice things for her almost from the day he'd moved in. Including offering to be her silent partner in Sweet Susie's Pastries and More. While he was gone, she'd mulled it over in her mind in between worrying about Audrey. In fact, Audrey's brush with illness only served to remind her life was short and precious. Heaven knew her father's life was cut short. Now, was the time for her to act. If Casey wanted to be her partner, why shouldn't she take him up on it? Why not go all in to secure stability for Ally and herself? She'd hoped to discuss it with him tonight to give him her answer, but he was clearly exhausted. He hadn't seemed himself when he'd come home. Tomorrow, after he was well rested, they would have a chance to talk.

Just as she opened Casey's refrigerator door, music rang out from another room. She jumped and fumbled with the dish in her hands, catching it before it crashed to the floor. She froze and spun around to Ally, putting two shushing fingers to her lips.

Ally's hand flew to her mouth to cover another round of giggles.

Then Susie heard the rich baritone sound of Casey's voice.

Casey jerked from sound sleep to an upright position on the sofa when his phone rang. He groped for his cell on the side table and knocked into a whiskey bottle. The damn thing tipped and he caught it just in time. He set it next to his shot glass. The two of them had been fast friends a few hours ago.

"Hello."

"Casey, it's Audrey."

His mind sobered up quickly. "Audrey, is anything wrong?"

"No, no. I'm home now, in my own bed. And feeling better. The anesthesia has worn off and I'm on pain meds now, but nothing too strong."

"Okay, that's good to hear."

"Actually, I'm calling about you."

"Me, honey? Why?"

"Well, uh, once my head cleared of all the fog, I started to remember our conversation at the hospital."

"And?"

"Well, your eyes lit up when we were talking about Susanna. You had this look on your face, Casey. Sort of like the look I get when I'm talking about Luke. And you called her Suse. I don't know, it sounded so sweet."

Casey stilled and rose from his seat. He stared unseeing out the living room window. Audrey was hitting too close to home. "Susanna is a sweet woman, Audrey. What are you getting at?"

"Are you falling for her?"

"No, I'm not falling for Susanna." It was a bend of the truth. Casey had already fallen for her. "Look, Audrey. I'm here on your suggestion to help her out, make life a little easier for her. That's my mission. And I've done that in every way I could figure. I had to get close to her to do it. I've almost got her convinced to partner with me on her shop. After that, I don't know where else I can go from there."

Something crashed. It sounded like glass from behind him. Coming from his kitchen? He turned sharply. Oh, crap! Susie was standing in his doorway surrounded by splintered glass. A dish? There were pieces of, chicken and a mess of gravy all over the floor. Her face…*ah, hell*. Her face was twisted in shock, crimson flushing her cheeks. Her shoulders were rigid enough to hold up the house. Hatred, pain and despair blackened her eyes. In the background, he heard Ally whimpering.

"Audrey, I'll call you back." Casey shut down the phone and flung it onto the sofa.

"Stay there, Ally," Susie said to the child, who was still in the kitchen out of his line of sight.

She marched over to him and raised her arm. Flesh met flesh as she slapped his face. The sting burned his cheek and traveled down to his toes. Her eyes flared. "I'll tell you where else you can go, Casey. Straight to hell."

"Susie, listen. It's not what you think." He reached for her.

She wiggled away from his grasp. "Not another word. I have to get Ally home. She's upset now."

Oh, God. Ally? Casey clamped his mouth shut. Ally

didn't need to hear this. She didn't need to bear witness to the two of them fighting. And that's what it would be, a horrible argument. Casey couldn't really defend himself to her anyway. "Okay, okay. I'll call you later."

Susie had already turned her back on him. "Don't you dare."

Then she marched into his kitchen, stepping over broken glass, and slammed the back door behind her.

Curses spattered from his mouth, but they wouldn't help relieve or repair anything. Inside, a dull ache grew, a slow growing infestation that would spread and kill any joy he'd had in his heart. He could only imagine what Susie was thinking right now. What pain she was going through. The words she'd overheard hurt her terribly. But he couldn't tell her what she needed to hear. He couldn't say, I love you and then walk away from her. He couldn't add to the hurt. He wasn't the right man for Susie. He couldn't give her the life she wanted.

What had she been doing in his house anyway? Why had she used her key to come inside the back door? He spied a piece of paper stuck on the refrigerator door. Skirting the broken glass and food on his kitchen floor, he reached for it and lifted the lavender parchment from underneath a magnet. It read: *Your favorite, because you're my favorite...just in case you get hungry tonight.*

"Susie." He rolled his shoulder around, allowing the refrigerator to hold him up. Bringing the note close, he clutched it tight to his chest and clunked the back of his head against cool stainless steel. His eyes misted and a long winding snake of despair began to squeeze the breath from his lungs.

Ten

Susie held it together long enough to put Ally down to sleep. She'd managed to persuade the little sweetheart that everything was fine. Ally was sensitive. She picked up on things. A distressed tone of voice was enough to send her into a panic. Part of that came from being a child, but another part of that came from Ally's wretched past. Lord knew, Susanna had been aware of all that before she'd taken Ally into her home.

Her goal was to provide Ally with a stable life. One where she wouldn't have to be afraid anymore. Susie had to be her rock. She couldn't let the child see her fall apart. Seeing her drug-addicted mother's decline on a daily basis had been enough.

Susie tiptoed out of Ally's bedroom. All evening, she'd thought a glass of wine would calm her trembling nerves, but she'd lost that desire along with everything else. Her heart bled now.

After keeping a stiff upper lip for Ally, Susie was free to sink down on her own bed fully clothed and let the tears spill down her cheeks.

Casey's brutal words sliced her up inside. Her silent cries turned to sobs. She covered her mouth to keep the pathetic sound from reaching Ally's ears. How could something as intangible as words gut her so perfectly? How could they instill such inconsolable sadness? Energy seeped from her every pore. She felt it leave her body until numbness took over. It was a luxury to let her emotions bleed this way. Tomorrow, for Ally's sake, she would have to put on a brave face. Yet, one thing kept bothering her. One thing went unanswered.

Why had Casey done it? Didn't he know how devastated she'd be to learn the truth?

Suddenly, she hinged up on the bed. She vowed he wouldn't get away with hurting her a second time. The last time she'd been rebuked by him, she'd trotted away like a dog with its tail between its legs. She'd simply gone off and licked her wounds, never to forget.

This time had to be different. She wouldn't let him get away with destroying her, without hearing from her, without letting her defend herself. Without giving her the chance to ask *why?*

She rose and headed to the kitchen in search of her phone. She found it facedown on the counter with the ringer shut off. With a press of a button, her screen lit up. She'd had three calls and two text messages from Casey. He wanted to explain. He wanted to talk to her. He asked her to pick up the phone.

Damn him.

Come to the back door, she texted him back. And be quiet, Ally is sleeping. I have questions.

Not five minutes later, after Susie had washed up and reapplied some light makeup to hide her teary face, she let Casey into her house.

"Thanks for seeing me."

His eyes, so clear and gorgeous blue, held sincere concern. Was that supposed to make her feel better?

She led him into the kitchen, which was the room farthest from Ally's. "Sit down, Casey." She pointed to a chair.

This had to be on her terms. She was broken up inside, but at least she had this.

He sat.

She paced for a minute and as she counted her footfalls, praying to keep from crying, he followed her every movement. Normally, she liked having his eyes on her, touching her in appreciative ways without laying a hand on her. Had it all been a lie?

"I need you to tell me the truth," she said, swallowing her pride.

Casey closed his eyes briefly, and then nodded as he opened them. "I never meant to hurt you in any way, Susie. At first, I hoped you wouldn't find out. Then after," he said, his gaze roving over her body like a hot torch, "I wanted to come clean and tell you, but things just got…" He sighed. "Heavy."

Her eyes burned as she fought tears. "Did you think of yourself as Robin Hood or something? I mean, now that I think about it…I realize how oblivious I've been. All those gifts, the things you provided for me and Ally."

"Not all that much," he said adamantly. "I wish I could've done more."

"I'm not a charity case, for heaven's sake!"

"Don't you think I know that?"

"No, I don't know that. It's what you do, Casey. Isn't it? At the Think Pink Strong awards, you didn't want credit for anything. You're generous, that much I can say." Except when it counted the most…with his heart. "And you don't want anyone to know about your contributions. Okay, I get that with cancer research. But with me? That's what I don't understand. Why'd you really come to Reno?"

"I had business here. I had to oversee the final stages of the restaurant and see to Sentinel's expansion in Reno. All that is true, Susie."

"But nothing else was." Her shoulders fell and she heard the bravado go out of her voice.

Casey lowered his head and pinched the bridge of his nose. "You've had a rough time even before Ally came to live with you." He paused. "Your folks…they took my sister in and cared for her when I couldn't. They fed her, helped her with homework, took her to ball games, made sure she had everything she needed. I couldn't have raised Audrey without their help. Is it so wrong of me to want to repay that kindness?"

Susie stared as the muscles in his left cheek twitched. "Oh, my God. I understand now. What a fool I've been. All this time, you were only leading me on. Making me believe you wanted to help me because…you cared about me. Now I see the truth. None of this came from your heart. You were only helping me to settle some sort of *debt* you think you owe my parents?"

"I wouldn't put it that way."

"What way would you put it? You deceived me. You insinuated yourself into our lives…mine and Ally's, when you knew how vulnerable she was. You lied to me over and over."

"I never lied."

"You made me believe that you cared about me." Her voice was beginning to crack and she made a special point of taking steady breaths to keep calm. "But you don't. I was an obligation to you. Something you could check off your guilt list."

His beautiful mouth twisted defiantly. "I do care about you."

"You made love to me, Casey. I thought we had something special. Don't you get it? You betrayed me in the worst possible way. You seduced me to get me to take you on as a partner. You must've thought I was such an easy target." Sick laughter slipped out and her voice rose in pitch.

She sounded like a mental case. "After all, I gave up my virginity for you the first time. What's a little deception between neighbors now?"

He rose and pointed his finger toward her. "That's not true, Susie. It was never like that between us. I separated the two, in my head. Is it so hard to believe I wanted you for you?"

She bounded from her chair too, facing him across the table. "Yes, it's damn hard to believe that when I overhear you telling your sister you're *not* falling for me. You were on some sort of mission. Gee, you'd run out of ideas as to how to next deceive me. What am I supposed to think? How can I believe anything you say? And how much of this was Audrey's idea? I'm not too thrilled with her right now either."

"Audrey doesn't know anything about us. She only had good intentions."

"Unlike you. You used me, Casey. To get what you wanted. You never thought I could manage Sweet Susie's on my own. By helping me in business, what? Your conscience would be clear? You could leave here and feel you paid your debt to the Hart family." She paused. It was hard to get the last words out, but she had to say them. "So you could wash your hands of me."

She turned her head away, attempting to hold back the flood of tears.

"Ah, Suse. Don't cry. Please."

Casey reached for her but she quickly stepped back, her shoes scuffing the linoleum. If he touched her, she didn't know what she would do. "Don't." Shaking her head, tears leaked from her eyes. "Don't, Casey."

Thankfully, he stopped at her command. "I'm so sorry, sweetheart."

"I. Am. Not. Your. Sweetheart."

Casey blew out an exasperated sigh.

"Needless to say, I'm not going into business with you."

She wished she could remove the new fencing and strip the paint off the patio cover. But most of all, she wished she could wipe away the memory of making love with him.

"Susie, I was only trying to help you."

"Helping me would be to ask me if I needed anything. Helping me would be to offer something upfront. Helping me isn't screwing me in the middle of the night to muddle up my brain and get me to agree to your terms."

His eyes flickered in disapproval. "Susie."

There was warning in his tone but it didn't deter her. If anything, it gave her a small measure of consolation to annoy him.

"You *screwed* me, Casey…in more ways than I can name. I think we're through here. You've answered all my questions." She folded her arms and took a stand. He wouldn't dare come near her.

"I really do care for you, Suse. You have to believe that," he began. "You're an amazing woman, smart, pretty, dedicated."

She snorted, but oblivious Casey didn't notice.

"In trying to help you, things got out of hand. But I only had your welfare at heart. I'm not…"

"What?"

He paused, probably thinking better of saying anything else. He'd said enough. Or rather, he hadn't said the words she'd desperately wanted to hear. He hadn't tried to fix anything.

"As I said, we're through here."

"What about…" His eyes softened. "What about Ally?"

"Ally?" Just the way he said her name gave her goose bumps. It could've been so great for the three of them but she knew what he was getting at. Ally was attached to the dog. She'd grown fond of Casey, too. It nearly destroyed Susie to think Ally would have another disappointment in her life because she'd misjudged Casey. She hadn't protected the child the way she should have. Both of them would feel heartache now. "I'll think of something."

"I'll let Charger into your backyard in the afternoons so Ally can play with him. If that's okay."

"That's fine for now."

She stood like a rock and refused to look his way. After a minute, he got the hint and walked past her toward the door. "I'm really sorry about hurting you, Susie."

She shrugged and whispered, "What else is new," before the door closed behind him.

Morning crept into his room, shedding unwanted sunshine on his face, and Casey grimaced. He had the mother of all headaches today. He rubbed his forehead briskly and knew it wouldn't wipe away the effects of his hangover.

Man, he hadn't tied one on like that since his rodeo days.

Except last night, he drank alone.

And felt like crap this morning.

Susie's shocked face kept replaying in his mind, like it had for the past three days.

He missed her like crazy. She was only one house away, but his neighbor and one-time friend didn't want anything to do with him. Every afternoon, as promised, he'd let Charger into her backyard. A few times, he'd heard Ally playing with the dog, her contagious giggles affecting his heart. He missed Ally, too.

He'd only gotten a brief glimpse of Susie once since the night she'd broken it off with him. Yesterday afternoon she'd been bringing Ally inside as the sun slipped beyond a pine tree in Susie's backyard. He'd been at the gate, ready to call the dog back home. She'd startled at seeing him. Weariness plagued her pretty features and Casey cursed himself for getting involved with her in the first place. He was convinced he wasn't the right man for her.

"Hello, Susie," he'd said from over the gate.

"Casey." She held her chin high, but he'd heard sadness in her voice.

"Charger poked a hole in our ball," Ally had announced.

Casey had smiled. "Did he now?"

She'd nodded. "He went arggh." She'd scrunched up her face and had pretended to take a bite out of an imaginary ball.

He'd laughed.

Ally had faced him from ten feet away, her head at a tilt, her innocent eyes meeting his. "Can you come over?" the little girl had asked.

Susie's nose had wrinkled. "Casey's busy tonight, Ally. Thank him for letting us play with Charger. We have to go in now."

"Thank you," she'd said politely.

Susie had ushered Ally into the house before Casey had time to say, "You're welcome."

The bittersweet memory forced him out of bed. His head spun as he rose to his feet. He took a breath and then another, tunneling fresh oxygen into his lungs. He needed to get a grip on reality. His heart weighed heavily as he came to the conclusion that leaving Reno and making a clean break was the only solution. For Susie and Ally. It had to be done.

He'd managed to conclude his work here for now. But he did have one more thing to do.

He glanced at the clock. It was after nine already. He dialed his sister's number and she answered on the first ring. "Morning, Audrey. How are you feeling today?"

"I'm fine, Casey. Except my bestie is a little angry with me."

"She shouldn't be. You didn't foul up, I did. I should've never gotten involved with her."

"Then why did you? And why did you lie to me about it?"

"I'm sorry, sis. I wasn't ready to talk about Susie to anyone, especially you, since it might've put you in the middle of a tough situation. As for Susie, my feelings for her kinda just crept up on me. It wasn't expected or intentional. It just happened."

"Susie sounded miserable when we talked the other day, Case. She was trying to hide her pain, because that's what she does. She never complains. And she's got all this pride. But I think she's in love with you. And I think you're in love with her. Are you denying that?"

Casey winced. The truth of her words stung. He did love Susie. With all of his heart. But to hear his little sis say that Susie loved him…well now, that was all the more reason to head home and spare her any more pain. "I'm not denying a thing, honey. I want you to trust me on this. It's impossible." He wouldn't allow Susie to make another sacrifice in her life, for him. "I'm coming home, Audrey. But before I do, I want your blessing on my decision."

"I would rather you didn't sell the house, Casey. You know how I feel about that."

"You're not living here anymore. I damn well won't be welcome here again. There's no use hanging on to a place neither of us wants or needs."

"You don't have to do it now," she said softly.

"Maybe I do," he answered in a gravelly voice. His throat constricted. "Maybe I need to let go of this place once and for all."

"Oh, Casey. I'm so sorry. Do whatever you think is best."

After he hung up with his sister, he set a pot of coffee to brewing and ten minutes later, downed two steaming cups one right after the other. Now, if his damned head would clear and the ache in his gut would disappear, he might get something accomplished today.

At eleven o'clock, Lana Robards showed up for their appointment, right on schedule.

She gave him an odd look when he let her into the house.

He looked like hell and he knew it. He'd showered, but hadn't shaved or combed his hair. He wore gray sweats but she looked like the doggone Duchess of Windsor in a classy white jacket and a matching skirt tight enough to raise eyebrows. She'd completed the look with long chain necklaces and high heels.

He offered her a seat at the dining room table.

She drew up the papers and smiled at him a number of times. She went over sales figures and neighborhood comps and explained everything in a professional manner. The lady knew her stuff. When she was through and all the papers were signed, she brought her head up to search his eyes once more. "Are you sure about this, Casey?"

He paused. Was he? He'd raised Audrey in this house. It had been just the two of them for years and there were some good memories here. But how could he come back here again? How could he see Susanna and Ally and not want to be with them.

You screwed me in so many ways.

Susanna hated him right now. She'd never forgive him a second time. They had no future together.

"I'm sure."

She leaned forward, the tops of her breasts pushing together under the material of her soft silk blouse. "That's a shame," she said softly. "It might have been nice getting to know you better."

Sexy. But not for him. He looked into her almond-shaped eyes. "That would've been nice, but I'm leaving tomorrow. I don't think I'll be back around this way much."

Except that he would have offices in Reno now. If he decided to stay the night, he'd use the corporate condo he'd recently leased for business executives and clients, well away from Meadow Drive.

"Okay, well…I appreciate your business. The For Sale sign will go up this afternoon."

He nodded and they both stood.

"Thank you."

"Sure."

He splayed his hand on her back and ushered her out the front door and down the steps. As soon as sunshine hit his face, he squinted and gazed across his lawn. Susie stood at her mailbox, reaching inside. She turned when she heard voices and saw them together. Her eyes dropped down to his hand on Lana's back. Slowly, he removed it.

It was too late.

There was an accusatory look in Susie's green eyes. Damning him.

Crap.

He was a genius at finding ways to hurt Susie.

She whipped around and hurried into her house before he or Lana could greet her properly. That conversation would've been awkward at best. But how could she think he'd have anything to do with Lana, when he wanted her—little Susanna Hart, his next-door neighbor, his sister's best friend—with an intensity that shocked him into self-sacrifice?

He said a swift goodbye to Lana and climbed up the steps of his house.

He needed a drink and coffee wasn't going to cut it.

Charger sure had a good life, snoring peacefully on the sofa. Casey envied him right now, having no cares in the world, no worries about doing what was right or wrong.

It was almost time to rouse him. Casey let the pup into Susie's yard every afternoon around four o'clock. It was Ally's playtime and he didn't want to disappoint the little girl, today of all days.

Casey's hands fisted tight. His heart squeezed tighter. He'd spent the afternoon making last minute arrangements, tying up loose ends and trying to figure out how to say goodbye to Susie and Ally. One thing he knew for certain—he wasn't leaving without seeing both of them and wishing them well. Hopefully, Susie had prepared Ally and explained that this day would eventually come, but man, oh man, saying goodbye wasn't going to be easy.

Someone knocked briskly on his door. Charger lifted his head, his ears perked up and he began barking. The pup beat him to the front door. Casey expected to see someone from the Realtor's office regarding the For Sale sign when he opened the door.

"Mrs. Hart?" Suddenly, he was a teenager again, looking at the kindhearted face of his next-door neighbor.

"Hi, Casey."

She surveyed his miserable appearance from top to bottom. If possible, he looked worse than this morning when he was sporting a nasty hangover. A scruffy beard shadowed his face, his hair flopped and fell wherever it wanted and his clothes were wrinkled from lying in them all afternoon.

Immediately he straightened up. "It's good to see you."

She opened her arms and he walked into them. She'd been like a second mother to him. Her hug was genuine and heartfelt. Casey gave her an extra squeeze before letting her go.

"It's good to see you too, Casey. It's been too long."

"Do you want to come inside?"

She nodded without hesitation. "I do."

He stepped aside and scratched his ear as she walked into the living room. Eleanor Hart wasn't here on a friendly visit. She had a determined look in her eyes that made Casey shudder.

"Don't mind Charger. He's friendly, but if he bothers you, I'll put him outside." The dog had been sniffing her shoes since the moment he'd opened the front door. "Please have a seat."

Eleanor looked around the room with keen eyes and sat

down on the edge of the sofa facing the window. When he took a seat opposite her, she smiled sweetly. "Casey, you look terrible."

She was the only person who could deliver that line without fear of recourse. "I know."

"Susie has that same hollow, ridiculously empty look in her eyes."

Casey ran a hand down his face.

"I heard her voice on the phone the other day, and knew something was terribly wrong. I booked a flight and flew out here as soon as I could. I hope I'm not too late."

What could he say to that? "Too late?"

"Susie is heartbroken. When I arrived here, she told me only enough for me to figure out that she's in love with you. Terribly, terribly in love with you, Casey. And she's hurting. But she's not saying much. No, my Susanna has too much pride and moxie for that. For three years, I've been asking her if she'd like to move to Georgia. And for three years, she's been telling me no. Her home is here. She has friends. She has a business she loves. All of a sudden, yesterday, my Susie tells me she's thinking about moving. But I didn't hear that. I only heard the shallowness in her voice. I heard the spark and drive and joy gone from my sweet girl. Mind you, I'd love to have Susie and Ally living closer to me, if that's what Susie really wants. I know in my heart, it isn't."

"Maybe it would be best for Susie if she did move closer to you. She misses you."

Eleanor Hart lowered her head and gazed at him through upturned eyes. It was the same look a teacher gave a student after making a bogus excuse for not doing his homework. "Casey, answer one question for me. Do you love my daughter?"

Casey never could lie to Mrs. Hart. He wasn't about to

start now. But his confession didn't come easily. He sighed and finally admitted, "Yes. I love Susie."

"I take it she doesn't know that."

"No, I haven't told her."

"Why not, Casey?"

Seconds ticked by. Mrs. Hart's gaze stayed vigilant on his face. "It's complicated."

"Is there another woman in the picture?"

He shook his head hard. "No."

"If she loves you and you love her, what's keeping you two apart?"

"You mean besides the fact that she won't even look at me right now?"

Eleanor leaned over to pat his hand. "You both could work that out. I know you tried to help her and it all went wrong. She thinks you led her on and betrayed her, but there are three little words out there that can mend a lot of broken hearts, Casey."

He shook his head. "Sometimes, that's not enough. Sometimes…there's something bigger that can't be fixed."

She gave him a thoughtful stare. "There's some sort of obstacle keeping you apart?"

He nodded. "Yeah."

"And Susie doesn't know?"

"No, Susie doesn't know. I'm afraid if I told her, she'd make a huge sacrifice for me. I can't let her do that. She deserves more."

"She deserves the truth from you, Casey. Believe me, I've learned that keeping secrets to protect someone isn't always the answer. When Susie's father was ill and we hid it from her, she was angry with us for a long time. Yes, she was young and we thought we had the right to spare our daughter the heartache. But in the long run, it wound up hurting her more. Casey, don't make the same mistake we made. Tell Susie the truth. She's a bright intelligent girl.

Whatever it is, she'll handle it. You can't leave her in the dark. She deserves more than that, don't you agree?"

He blew out a breath. "I'm leaving tomorrow."

"Were you going to put the house up for sale and then take off without saying goodbye?"

"No, I…" His brows rose. How did she know? He turned his head to gaze out the window behind him as a worker climbed into his truck and pulled away from the curb, leaving a prominent For Sale sign planted in the middle of his front lawn.

Eleanor went on. "I can watch Ally tonight, if you decide you'd like some time with Susie to talk it out."

"It's doubtful she'll talk to me."

"She'll talk to you. I'll make sure of that."

"How?"

Eleanor's reassuring smile touched him deep inside and filled the emptiness with hope. "I'm her mother. I have my ways."

The For Sale sign in front of Casey's house was the last nail in the coffin as far as Susie was concerned. She was determined to hold back her tears as she walked away from the kitchen window. That house had been a symbol of love and friendship between two families for years. How could Casey do this? She saw the selling of his house as a rebuke, a stinging slap in the face to all the memories their families shared. He truly was washing his hands of her. The more she fought tears and protected her injured heart, the deeper her despair. Her wounds were fresh and raw, still bleeding, and putting that sign up plunged a second knife into her.

She didn't want to speak to Casey at all, but her mother had convinced her she needed closure. She needed to get things off her chest and finally be free of him. He'd never cared about her. She'd been his duty, his obligation, a way to ease his conscience and unburden the guilt he'd lived with taking her virginity. All of that garbage made her sick inside. Instead of withering into a mass of pitiful emotions, Susie's strength would carry her through.

It had to.

She fixed her makeup and put on fresh clothes, a comfy pair of jeans and a simple butter-yellow blouse.

"Almost ready, Susie?" her mother asked, coming into her bedroom. "Oh, dear. You're not wearing that, are you, sweetheart?"

"I'm not dressing up for Casey." *Been there, done that.* "It's not a date."

Her mother opened the closet door and picked out a scoop neck sundress with feminine flowing lines in pastel tints of cotton candy pink, pistachio and iris. She hadn't worn the chiffon dress in a while. It reminded her of a French impressionist painting. "No, it's not a date." Her mother laid the dress on the bed. "But why not leave him with a memory he won't forget?"

"Mom!"

Her mother chuckled sweetly. "That's what your father would always tell me. Leave me with a memory, Eleanor."

Susie squeezed one eye shut and twisted her face. "TMI, Mom."

She chuckled again. "Your choice. Think about it. Casey will be here in a few minutes."

Her mother had set the whole thing up.

Ten minutes later, Susie faced Casey at the front door. Her mother and Ally had conveniently disappeared and it was just the two of them, standing on opposite sides of the threshold. Tonight he wore a black polo shirt tucked into beige trousers. No matter how he dressed, whether in cowboy duds or business tycoon casual, the sculpted planes on his face, his cerulean eyes and bronzed skin took her breath away. His hair was trimmed at the collar now and no stubble darkened his cheeks.

Dusk had settled over the trees, their branches casting shadows on the lawns. There was a pleasant warmth in the air. It was quiet on Meadow Drive this evening. Nothing stirred, except her crazy heart.

Casey stared at her, his eyes dropping a little to take in her dress. "You look beautiful, Susanna."

"Thank you." She was glad she'd taken her mother's advice.

"I thought we'd go for a drive to the river."

"Oh…" She'd thought they'd talk in his house. But what difference did it make really? "All right."

He walked beside her as they made their way toward his SUV parked in the driveway. He opened the passenger door and she slid in, immediately putting on her seat belt and facing forward. She caught the light scent of his cologne and unruly memories of hot nights under the sheets making uninhibited, erotic love flashed through her mind: Of his muscled body pressed to hers, the feel of him swelling inside her and making her dreams come true. Then the images of their sizzling limousine sex popped into her head, so dangerously exciting that nothing would ever compare. His scent reminded her of all those things.

Don't go there, Susie. Don't get sentimental now. Not when the man you've loved for ten years was packing up and leaving town for good.

He climbed into his seat, adjusted his seat belt and fired up the engine. He turned his head to her, his eyes two beacons of blue light. "I want you to know, nothing's going on between Lana and me."

He'd hit a nerve.

"It was business. She's a Realtor and—"

"It's none of *my* business, is it? You don't owe me an explanation, Casey."

Casey opened his mouth, his tongue working against his cheek, but then clamped his lips shut and gave a quick nod.

They continued the ride in silence all the way to the river.

Casey parked the car under a tree in a moonlit area on the banks of the Truckee.

"It's a nice night. Want to get out?"

"Yes." She needed to breathe fresh air and put space between them. She opened her door and stepped outside. He joined her by her side of the car. The gentle moonlight and quiet rush of the river soothed Susie's rattled nerves.

"I guess you saw the sign at the house," he began.

"I couldn't miss it."

He took a sharp breath. "I should have told you ahead of time. I'm sorry about that. It was a decision that was tough to make, but I figured it was best this way."

Grief thickened her throat. "Yes, it's for the best." She stared at the river.

Casey braced his hands on the car, leaning forward, his head hung low. It caught her attention. His brows drew together and he seemed to be struggling with something. "Your mother came to visit me today."

"I didn't send her over there, if that's what you're thinking." That would be the ultimate humiliation if he thought she'd sent her mom to plead her case.

He shook his head. "No. I know that. Eleanor...well, she's a pretty perceptive lady."

"How so?"

Casey sidled up close to take her hand in his. She let out a silent sigh of longing. God, how good he felt. His touch seeped through her body, warm, inviting and delicious. Instead of the ridiculous confidence she normally saw in his eyes, she witnessed pain and heartache. "Because she figured out that I was in love with you, Susanna."

Susie gulped oxygen. Had she heard correctly? It was the last thing she'd expected to hear. But if he loved her, why weren't they together? Why had he put his house up for sale? Why was he leaving?

He squeezed her hand and the pressure traveled straight to her heart. "I know I made a mess of things, but the truth is I think you're an amazing woman, an amazing mother. You're resourceful and hardworking and I've never admired a woman more. I surely didn't expect to fall in love with you. I didn't come here, looking for love or a relationship, but there you were, my next-door neighbor, giving me a hard time, making me earn your friendship again. Making me figure out unique ways to help you, because your pride and independent nature didn't make it easy for me."

"So I was a challenge?"

He smiled. "Hell, yeah, you were. In the beginning. But then you became so much more to me. Yes, I came here to help you get through some tough times, that's true. But you've also helped me in so many ways. You've shown me a sweeter side of life, Suse. I know now, what being a family really means. I'm deeply and wholly in love with you, Susanna. And Ally? God, I love that little girl."

"Oh, Casey." Everything inside her melted like rich, smooth icing flowing down a hot chocolate cake. "I never thought I'd hear those words from you."

"I was trying to protect you. I'm still trying to protect you."

She searched his eyes for the truth. "How are you protecting me? From what I overheard you saying to Audrey, you pretty much dismissed me as nothing more than an obligation."

He touched her face, his palm caressing her cheek tenderly. "I'm sorry. I wasn't thinking clearly. When I left you that night, I was determined to tell you how I felt about you when I returned, but then…"

"Then what? What happened? Why did you back off?"

He sighed deeply. "I realized I couldn't give you the

life you deserve. You've made a lot of sacrifices in the past. I didn't want you to have to make the biggest one of all for me."

"How would I be sacrificing for you, Casey?"

Sadness touched his eyes as his hand on her cheek fell away. "I know you want children of your own. Lots of them. The day I broke my back, I also lost the ability to have children. I'm sterile, honey."

She blinked. That was the reason he was leaving?

"I haven't told anyone about this, Susie."

Suddenly relieved, she kept her smile on the inside. "Except Audrey. You told her, didn't you?"

"Yes, but what does that—"

"She let it slip to me one day. It was shortly after your accident and Audrey felt so badly about it, that I promised her we'd never speak of it again. And we haven't."

"Are you saying that you've known all along?"

Susie began bobbing her head up and down. "Yes, I've known that all along, Casey. You're not telling me something new. I went into this with my eyes wide open."

"But, sweetheart. You want lots of children."

"Those were childhood fantasies of silly young girls. That's not my reality anymore. When we made love the first time, I wasn't some foolhardy girl giving up her virginity to a fantasy man, Casey. I've been in love with you since I was a teenager. I've always known what I wanted. Trust me, on this. Loving you, raising my sweet Ally and working at a business I enjoy is more than enough for me. Isn't it enough for you?"

"Hell, yes," he said immediately. The tortured look on his face transformed into a wide grin. "You're sure?"

"I'm positive."

Her feet left the ground and she found herself being twirled around in Casey's strong arms. The cool river air lifted her dress as she spun. When her feet finally found earth again, he rained dozens of kisses on her face. "I love you, Susie. I love you so much," he kept whispering in her ear, over her cheeks, on her forehead. Everywhere his mouth touched, he expressed his devotion.

Susie giggled and kissed him back until they were spent and out of breath.

Then Casey took a step back and landed on one knee on the hard packed ground. He reverently took her hand, his eyes glistening with emotion. "I love you more than a man has ever loved a woman. Susanna Hart, will you marry me? Will you allow me to be a part of your family?"

Tears dripped down her cheeks. She'd never been happier. "Yes, Casey Thomas, I will marry you."

Relief washed over his face. As if Susanna would ever refuse Casey's love. He rose then and drew her into his arms. "We'll have a great life, sweetheart. I'll build you a house in Tahoe with a newfangled kitchen or we can stay here in Reno and you can open your shop. Whatever you want to do is fine with me. My home is with you and Ally."

Susanna reached up on tiptoes and kissed him soundly on the lips. He tasted…happy. She smiled. "We'll figure it out, my love. We have forever."

"I can't wait to make you my wife." Casey grabbed her hand. "Let's go."

"So soon?" she asked. She wanted more time alone with him.

"Your mom didn't give you a curfew, did she?"

She shook her head.

Sizzling hunger entered his eyes. "I need to be alone with you. We can check into a hotel for a few hours. We'll get a penthouse suite. You deserve the very best."

She nibbled on her lower lip. "But I already have the very best. And we are alone." She leaned heavily against the back door of his SUV and smiled. "It's pretty remote out here, wouldn't you say?"

His brows gathered as he looked around the solitude of the riverbank. When he caught on, a dangerous grin lit his face. "Sweet Susie wants SUV sex?"

She nodded, her heart bursting with joy. "I want you anywhere, anytime. And the sooner the better."

Casey growled his approval and gallantly swept open the door to his backseat. "There's no way I'm going to let my fiancée down. Get in, sweetheart."

Susie climbed in and reached for Casey.

He would take her on a ride to last a lifetime.

* * * * *

If you loved REDEEMING THE CEO COWBOY,
pick up the other stories in
THE SLADES OF SUNSET RANCH *series*
from USA TODAY bestselling author
Charlene Sands

SUNSET SURRENDER
SUNSET SEDUCTION
THE SECRET HEIR OF SUNSET RANCH

All available now from Harlequin Desire!